I0590931

Like a Boss

A NOVELLA

A NOVELLA

International Bestselling Author

MONICA JAMES

LIKE A BOSS

This book is a work of fiction. Names, characters, places and incidents are the product of the author's imagination, or are used fictitiously. Any resemblance to actual events, locales, or persons living or dead, is coincidental. Any trademarks, service marks, product names or named features are assumed to be the property of their respective owners and are used only for reference.

Copyright © 2025 by Monica James

All rights reserved. No part of this work may be reproduced, scanned or distributed in any printed or electronic form without the express, written consent of the author.

Cover Design: Taywel Designs
Editing: My Brother's Editor
Formatting: Flutterby Formatting

Follow me on:
authormonicajames.com

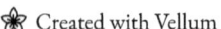 Created with Vellum

Other Books by

MONICA JAMES

THE I SURRENDER SERIES
I Surrender
Surrender to Me
Surrendered
White

SOMETHING LIKE NORMAL SERIES
Something like Normal
Something like Redemption
Something like Love

A HARD LOVE ROMANCE
Dirty Dix
Wicked Dix
The Hunt

MEMORIES FROM YESTERDAY DUET
Forgetting You, Forgetting Me
Forgetting You, Remembering Me

SINS OF THE HEART DUET
Absinthe of the Heart
Defiance of the Heart

ALL THE PRETTY THINGS TRILOGY
Bad Saint
Fallen Saint
Forever My Saint
The Devil's Crown-Part One (Spin-Off)
The Devil's Crown-Part Two (Spin-Off)

THE MONSTERS WITHIN DUET
Bullseye
Blowback

DELIVER US FROM EVIL TRILOGY
Thy Kingdom Come
Into Temptation
Deliver Us From Evil

IN LOVE AND WAR
North of the Stars
Fall of the Stars

REVENGE IS SWEET SERIES
Crybaby

HEART MEMORY TRANSFER DUET
Heart Sick
Love Sick

KISS OR KILL SERIES
Bad for You

Chapter One

"Bay, would you please stop fidgeting?"

"I can't help it," I gripe, shuffling in my seat and attempting to sit tall. "It's your fault for making me wear this damn torture device. How the hell am I supposed to breathe in this thing?"

"You're not." My best friend, Hannah Glenn, chuckles. "Besides, you look beautiful." She playfully tugs at a loose brunette curl that has slipped free from my jeweled hairclip.

"I most certainly will not look beautiful when I pass out from lack of oxygen." I rearrange my position, hoping the movement will liberate my lungs, but it only makes me wheeze like a ninety-year-old, emphysemic old man.

The taxi driver looks at me through the rearview mirror, attempting to hide his smile—good to know I look as ridiculous as I feel.

"This was a bad idea. Please remind me why I'm not running back to the safety of your apartment."

"Because," Hannah states, peering into her compact as she

adjusts her side chignon. "You need a night out. Not to mention, you need a night out of your sweatpants. It's been three months, Baylee." Snapping her compact shut, she holds up three fingers to emphasize her point. "I hate to sound like a broken record, but you need to move on. And by move on, I mean you need to have wild, hot sex with a random stranger," she concludes, her mouth filter totally nonexistent, just like always.

"You know I'm not into one-night stands, Han," I affirm with conviction.

"Well, you should be. You're young, hot, and single. Go out there and grab a tiger by the balls."

"No, thank you. I'm steering clear of all tigers... and their balls." I know she's trying to help, but she's not.

Sighing, I gaze out the window, bracing my forehead against the cool glass. I would rather get lost in the bright city lights than have to deal with the mess that is my life.

Three months ago, the love of my life broke my heart into a million teeny tiny pieces. I never believed in the cheesy cliché until it actually happened to me. Goes without saying, it destroyed my world.

Scott was my high school sweetheart, and up until three months ago, I believed he was my happily ever after. Turns out Scott's happily ever after differed from mine dramatically, as his HEA was between the legs of my ex-boss—the soulless succubus.

Sadly for me, I walked in on them in a very compromising position at a work function. At first, I wanted to believe he was just helping her find her shoes. But unless her shoes were wedged in her vagina, then what I saw was indeed the disgusting truth.

I packed up my belongings and left our apartment because no matter how much I loved him, I loved myself more. There was no way I was going to waste my future on someone who didn't want me. And I most certainly wasn't going to waste my future on someone who had no qualms screwing my boss.

The first few days, anger fueled my every thought.

"I was better off."

"I didn't need him."

"A leopard doesn't change its spots," and so on.

All these affirmations were my driving force to survive. However, when one week passed, and I missed him more than life itself, I realized that surviving this wasn't going to be as easy as I thought.

Hannah, however, was my voice of reason, reminding me in my moments of weakness that Scott was a lying, cheating asshole. She also reminded me of the fact that Scott had ruined everything I'd worked so hard for. Not only had he ruined my life, but he had also ruined my career, because after seeing my boss's lady parts, there was no way I could stomach looking at her in the same way ever again.

I really admired Audrey Denis. She was a thirty-five-year-old, smart, successful businesswoman who was attractive, in good shape and reeked of success—success she had worked hard for. She was someone I looked up to—someone I wanted to become. She was married but kept her private life just that. Too bad her private life included screwing my boyfriend.

So I am now not only homeless but jobless, as well. And that's what has me tugging on the tight bodice of my blue silk gown.

Hannah works at Fox Technologies, and luck was finally on my side when the boss of all bosses, Mr. Dylan Fox, was in the market for a new personal assistant. I'm a NYU business graduate, but we all have to start somewhere. And besides, I was hoping Mr. Fox would see my potential and I could work my way up the corporate ladder.

So I applied online, not expecting anything, but was pleasantly surprised when I got a call back two days later informing me that I was hired. I was ecstatic, hopeful my bad luck had finally changed, but Hannah then confessed she had left out the minor detail that my boss was a renowned asshole. To date, he's had fifteen personal assistants, all of which have quit, unable to deal with his controlling, overbearing ways.

This fact indeed killed my high, but desperate times call for desperate measures. I was sick of using Hannah's couch as my bed, and my savings was slowly dwindling to nothing but pennies. I had to put on my big girl panties and suck it up because I was desperate to get my life back on track.

"So, who's going to be here?" I ask, finally snapping out of my funk and turning to look at my best friend.

"Everyone will be," she replies with a smile.

"Is everyone including my boss?"

Hannah nods, a small frown tugging at her lips. "I do find it strange he hired you without even meeting you. I mean, he is a control freak and all."

"Maybe my resume just blew him out of the water?" I playfully suggest as a plausible explanation.

"Maybe," she agrees but doesn't look convinced. She drops it however. "I thought this was a perfect opportunity for you to meet everyone you're going to be working with. And besides, tonight is a charity event, so everyone will be feeling... charitable."

"You know what, Han? Save the pep talks."

She smirks and claps excitedly. "I can't wait until we work together. It's only been our dream since we were ten years old."

I nod because she's absolutely right. But I have to get through tonight first before I even contemplate starting my new job on Monday.

When the cab pulls up a few feet away from the venue, we

slide out gradually, as our body-hugging dresses prevent much movement. While Hannah pays the driver, I look up at the vast, impressive *Hotel Du Luc* and whistle.

My cheeks are kissed by the crisp night breeze the moment we hit the sidewalk. *Hotel Du Luc* is classically aged and the bright lights outside highlight the undeniable sophistication inside. I've never seen anything so fancy, but I guess it's a sight I'll have to become accustomed to seeing as my boss demands nothing but the best.

We walk up the stairs, ready for whatever the evening decides to throw our way. The moment we enter the regal foyer, a sharply dressed middle-aged man with eagle eyes catches Hannah by the arm.

"You look ravishing, Hannah. Who's your friend?"

Hannah removes her arm from his grip. "My friend is someone who's been warned to stay away from you, Handsy Hugo."

My mouth hinges open at her blunt reply, but Handsy Hugo grins, appearing to be accustomed to Hannah's sass. "Save me a dance."

"Not a chance in hell," she replies over her shoulder, dragging me into the majestic ballroom.

I'm unable to appreciate the beauty around me because I'm too shocked by Hannah's blatant insolence. "*Who* was that?" I hook my thumb over my shoulder while Hannah shivers in disgust.

"That was the office pervert, that's who."

I screw up my nose. "Oh, duly noted. I will make sure to stay away from him."

Hannah grins her troublesome, dimpled smile. "Or, on second thought, maybe Handsy Hugo is exactly what you need."

I choose to ignore her, as I know she'll make it happen if I give it half a thought. A waiter zips past, and I steal a glass of champagne off the silver tray.

"Not listening, Hannah."

Before she has time to rebuke, a pretty girl of similar age to us runs over. "Han! Thank God you're here. I was about to fall asleep in the canapes. Who's this?" she asks, gesturing my way.

"Hey, Bonnie. This is Baylee Young."

Her jaw hits the ground. "Oh, you poor thing." She shakes her head sympathetically, but she soon recovers when she senses my confusion.

I turn to look at Hannah, wondering if she's shared my sob story with the entire office. The random girl sees my annoyance and quickly clarifies. "You're Mr. Fox's new personal assistant, right?"

Hannah smiles sweetly at me while I shake my head at her jab. "Yes, I am. So, why poor me?" I ask, downing my champagne in one big gulp.

Bonnie looks at Hannah, who shrugs. "She already knows what a pain in the ass he is."

Bonnie breathes out a sigh of relief, appearing thankful she wasn't the one who spilled the beans. "Pain in the ass is giving him a compliment. He's lucky he's so ridiculously hot because what he's lacking in the personality department, he sure makes up for look-wise." She fans herself while Hannah nods in agreement.

I gulp. Who the hell am I working for?

I steal Hannah's champagne and toss it down quickly.

Bonnie sees my anxiety and quickly amends. "I guess he's not *that* bad."

"No, he's worse," Hannah adds, chuckling when I stop the waiter for another glass of champagne. "Lighten up, Bay. At least you've got some eye candy to look at, no matter how bitter that candy may be. Bonnie and I are stuck looking at Handsy Hugo all day."

Both girls shudder while I laugh. Although, I don't know how long I'll be laughing as my boss sounds like the devil reincarnate.

"If you'll excuse me, I need to use the restroom," I say, as three glasses of champagne in the span of two minutes is my limit.

I go in search of the bathrooms but soon become disoriented because this place is like a damn maze, and these pumps are definitely not making my journey any easier. I make my way up the plush carpeted steps, but I don't have time to admire my superb surroundings as my bladder is about to burst. I sing in relief when I see the bathrooms are a few feet ahead.

Very ungracefully, I half run, half waddle, not caring I resemble a deranged duck because the only thing I care about is making it to the restrooms in time.

However, when I'm only mere steps away, my monster stilettos catch on the long hem of my gown and I clumsily trip over my own feet. I yelp, "Sweet baby Jesus!" and bump straight into a wall... of muscle.

Lifting my eyes up and... up, I see my muscled wall is attached to the hottest man... ever. And that hot man is smirking at me, his fingers searing my skin as he caresses my bicep with poise. My body goes lax, my mouth gapes open on its own accord, and my eyes go to town on the tall, dark, and handsome in front of me.

His eyes are incredibly bright, appearing a green-blue, licked with a curving swirl of violet. Their vibrancy complements his slightly down-turned lips, which gives him a full, sexy pout. His strong jawline is coated in a dark scruff, a dark scruff that matches his thick, wild tresses, styled messily atop his gorgeous head.

It's impossible that a man this hot actually exists. But as I rake my gaze down his hardened, chiseled physique, I know that it's possible, very possible.

Even underneath the monkey suit, I can see that he's the owner of a well-oiled machine, a machine which has me forgetting my own name. And obviously my manners, because when he clears his throat, I realize I'm staring at his groin.

"You're welcome," I blurt out. What the actual hell? That is so not what I intended to say.

But my stranger chuckles, a deep, gruff laugh, and goose bumps instantly bathe my skin.

"I mean, thank you," I correct a second later, feeling my cheeks rival the pinkness of his devious mouth. "I tripped over my shoes because I was busting to pee." Again, what the actual hell?

I need to shut up, but my need to fill the silence is greater and I continue rambling like a crazy person.

"Thank you for coming to my rescue. I can only imagine what compromising position I would be in if not for your skilled... hands." I cringe while my stranger smirks, a dimple hugging his whiskered cheek.

Why isn't he talking? He needs to talk, so I shut the hell up.

But when he strokes over my bicep once again, talking is the last thing on my mind.

He leans in close, his cologne encasing me in a prison of perfumed heaven. Does heaven have a smell? Well, it does now.

"After you're done..." he whispers, his voice deep, rough, and raw. "How about you come up to my room, and I'll show you how skillful my hands can really be."

I actually choke on my saliva and subtly cough so I can breathe. Is this man asking me what I think he's asking me? I mean, maybe he's a massage therapist, and he wants to knead the knots from my shoulders because God knows, the stress from the past three months has me wearing my shoulders for earrings.

However, when he leans in even closer and his lips tickle my ear, I know the only massaging he'll be doing is to my libido. "Just in case we're unclear... that was an invitation to fuck you senseless."

Before I have time to reply, he pulls away, appearing calm and composed, while I resist the urge to not vomit all over his expensive Italian loafers.

"Room fifteen thirty-five. See you soon," he confidently says before sauntering off with a self-assured swagger.

I stand frozen to the spot, my need to pee long gone because I have just been hit on by the world's *hottest* man, whose arrogance and self-assurance was a surprisingly heady combination. This has never happened to me before. I have always been with Scott. And when I say *been*, I mean that physically, as well as emotionally.

But just thinking about what that dirty son of a bitch did to me has me springing into action, ready to make good on Hannah's suggestion and grab a tiger by the balls. The thought of being naked and in his presence, however, has me yelping and running into the bathroom.

Once I'm done in the stall, I wash my hands and stare into the mirror above the sink. I look flustered, even more so than usual because my usual rosy cheeks rival a tomato. Dousing my neck with some water, I take three calming breaths.

Any sane woman would forget she just encountered this arrogant asshole and go back to the party. But I never said I was sane. And going back downstairs has every fiber in my body protesting loudly.

Fanning my cheeks, I hope it'll also douse the fire in my pants, but all it does has me remembering those mesmerizing eyes which could promise the world. The old Baylee would walk away because she would *never* do something so... spontaneous. But that Baylee got treated like a doormat by her supposed "soulmate."

With that as my incentive, I march out of the bathroom, making a beeline for the elevator. The doors part open, and I enter, refusing to back down.

"You are *not* a coward," I chant to myself for the sixth time, hoping the avowal will magically give me the confidence I so need.

It doesn't because I have ridden in the elevator to the fifteenth floor three times, and each time, I've ridden it back down to the lobby, unable to take that first step because I know I'll have to take another and then another after that.

I've never been the one-night stand kind of girl, and even though I've been in a relationship for the majority of my adult years, I still think that fact would stand, even if I hadn't been.

But it's not every day a girl like me gets propositioned on her way to the bathroom by a man who could have any woman he wanted.

I've always considered myself cute rather than beautiful. I've always been the pretty brunette with too many freckles on her nose, while Hannah was the leggy blonde beauty everyone wanted to screw. And I'm okay with that. Scott loved me for who I was. Well, I thought he did because I now know that Scott was a fucking liar.

Anger replaces my heartache, and before I know it, I'm in the elevator once again, riding it up to the fifteenth floor and storming down the hallway. "You are *not* a coward," I repeat for the final time before knocking on the door of room 1535.

Who was I kidding? I am *such* a coward. I was insane to think I could actually go through with this because the pounding of my heart and the shortness of breath reveals I'm moments away from having a heart attack.

But it's too late. Just as my common sense kicks in, the door opens, and before me stands my handsome stranger.

I gulp.

He smirks.

I gulp once again.

"Hello again." His voice is as smooth as velvet, his composure untroubled and calm as he leans against the doorjamb.

I, on the other hand, can feel the perspiration gathering on my brow.

This was a mistake, but as he steps aside, indicating I'm to enter, my feet act before my brain can protest and I'm trapped in the lion's, or should I say, tiger's den. I take a quick look around and can't deny the room is really beautiful and lavish. I have no doubt that money isn't an issue for my tiger.

When I hear the door close, I nervously spin around to see my stranger braced up against the wood grain, watching me with those intense eyes. Under his heated gaze, I feel naked and utterly exposed. I quickly check to ensure there are no wardrobe malfunctions.

When I'm in the clear, I meet his stare once again but am shocked to see a small grin tug at his full lips. I don't know why it shocks me, but my tiger appears like someone who doesn't let his guard down often.

"Would you like a drink?" he asks, pushing off the door, walking brashly toward me.

I slowly back away, only stopping when my calves hit the edge of a glass coffee table. "Um, sure. Thanks."

He nods, that damn cocky smile still plastered to his glorious face as he makes his way over to the refrigerator.

I watch with interest as he reaches for two wine glasses, pouring us a splash of red. I wish I knew what he was thinking because at the moment, he's keeping his cards close to his chest. Oh, and what a chest it is.

I thought I was here to be 'fucked senseless,' but maybe he was joking. Maybe he's actually a creepy pervert who lured me up here with the promise of sex, but instead, he's going to cut me up into itty bitty pieces and mail my remains to my mom and dad.

"I shouldn't be here," I confess, hating how my rationality decides to kick in *now*, because *now* is too late.

"Why not?" he coolly questions, both wineglasses in hand as he makes his way toward me. I haven't moved an inch.

"Because, I, er..." I fumble over my words because I don't even know what to say. Are you a serial killer, seems a little wrong.

"Because why?" he presses, handing me my wine.

I reach for the glass, ensuring our fingers don't touch. "Because I don't usually do this. Like ever. This isn't me." When he remains quiet, studying me closely, I add, "I'm sorry if I misled you downstairs."

He cocks his head to the side, his tongue darting out to wet his lower lip. He doesn't say anything, however, he simply watches me like prey.

His intensity would usually scare or intimate me, but coming from him, in a weird, unexplained way, it turns me on. I've never had a man look at me this way, and I dare say after tonight, I'll never experience it thereafter.

"You didn't mislead me. I know what your body wants... even if you don't." He finally speaks, although I think I preferred him mute.

I can't deny he's right. I can feel an unexpected dampness pooling in my underwear, a feeling I haven't experienced in a very long time. But can I really do this? Can I have a one-night stand with a complete and utter stranger who is extremely cocky and seems like a self-assured asshole?

With his gaze still firmly affixed to me, he runs a hand

through his dark brown hair, the longer layers on top sliding through his fingers effortlessly. I dig my fingernails into my palm to stop myself from reaching out and touching that tousled mess myself. Even though he is perfectly refined and reeks of class, his bed hair and three-day growth show me otherwise. Underneath this perfect getup, I sense a bad boy just waiting to emerge when the time and situation is just right.

Like right now.

He slowly loosens the black tie from around his thick neck, his eyes never wavering from mine when he unknots it. He unfastens the top button of his crisp white shirt, it pops open, adding to his rebellious look.

Wrapping the tie around his palm, he pulls the length, the action making me go weak at the knees. I've never been bound before but watching the way his long fingers tug at the material has me quickly wondering what it would feel like.

"Like what you see?" He laughs, the sound slightly mocking, mixed with a hint of curiosity.

His confidence suddenly ticks me off, and my stubbornness takes control. "I've seen better."

He has the nerve to laugh again and this time, the sound is filled with nothing but smugness. "Have you now?"

I nod, folding my arms over my chest to hide my mounting breaths.

"Once again, Bluebird, your body tells me otherwise."

"What are you talking about?" I ask, deciding to ignore the fact he just called me Bluebird.

"Well," he replies, taking another step toward me, while I step around the coffee table and take two back. "I dare say you're thinking about what I said to you downstairs. I think right now, right this second..." He pauses and breathes in evenly. "I think you're fantasizing about all the wicked and utterly despicable things I want to do to you."

Internally, I've just combusted, but I'll be damned if I let it show. "Well, I hate to rain on your ego parade, but you're wrong."

"No, I'm not," he counters with a self-righteous smile.

"Ah, yes, you are. It's my body; I think I know what it's capable of."

My dark stranger shakes his head, his eyes sizzling with challenge. "You have no idea what that hot body is capable of."

"You're an arrogant asshole," I bite back, hating how he knows me and my body so well.

He shrugs his massive shoulders, appearing undisturbed by my abuse. "I've been called worse. You know I'm right," he contests, cocking a dark brow.

"Are not," I childishly retort.

"Prove it then."

"Prove what?"

"Prove that your pussy is not deliciously slick and wet."

I gasp, his dirty words making me even wetter.

What is the matter with me? His huge ego should have me running for the door. But instead, I find myself wanting to accept his challenge because I know I'll lose. And I want to know what happens when I'm proven wrong.

"That's it, Bluebird. Let go. Let go of all the conventional notions of what's right and what's wrong. Just enjoy the moment of two people giving in to the most basic, most primitive emotion a human being can experience."

"And what's that?" I'm almost too afraid to ask.

Tiger smirks, unfastening a button and then another. "How about I just show you?"

My traitorous head nods, all reasoning going out the door the moment he drops his shirt to the floor, revealing his toned, sculpted chest. I've never been a fan of cleanly shaven men, as I like a bit of scruff. But the only scruff on my stranger is the scruff that paints his navel.

Muscles and rock-hard abs are usually not my thing, but now that I'm confronted with all of the above, I'm a complete convert. I could bounce pennies off his stomach and watch them spring back.

"*Now* do you like what you see?" he inquires, taking a step closer. This time, however, I don't retreat.

"Still not impressed," I whisper, my voice hoarse, betraying my internal war.

"You're a hard woman to please. Turn around," Tiger orders, his tone stern.

I do as he asks, thankful to have a moment to collect my thoughts without succumbing to those smoldering eyes.

My senses are on high alert, and I focus, eagerly awaiting his next move. The wait is unbearable, and just as I endeavor to turn around, his hand shoots out and ensnares me around the waist. Even though his touch is over my clothes, my skin feels like it's on fire. I whimper, shamefully wanting more.

He presses his firm chest against my back, his strength and warmth sheltering me in a comfortable, submissive state. He reads my submission and slowly glides his hand across my stomach, leaving an inferno in his wake. He's a lot taller than I am, therefore, I feel vulnerable and at his mercy. But I can't remember ever feeling so free.

The soft silk of my dress feels sinful as it slides up my leg, Tiger hitching it up higher and higher. Before long, my entire leg is exposed, and so are my drenched underwear. I'm grateful to be facing away from him because if Tiger could see me now, he'd know he's just proven me wrong.

Scott and I were never an adventurous couple in the bedroom. It was missionary, or from behind, and nothing else in between. He never went down on me, but he expected I go down on him. And like an idiot, I complied. But now, all I can think about is how Tiger's lips will feel between my thighs.

But first, it's his fingers I'll become accustomed to.

Slipping his hand between my legs, he rubs over the front of my underwear, my long dress partially draping his hand. I watch, mesmerized, as his cloaked fingers begin rubbing over me leisurely. It feels unbelievable, but I'm beyond mortified when a whimper escapes me, altering my proud Tiger that he's won.

"Told you," he whispers.

He bites my lobe as I lean my head back against his bare chest. I ignore his arrogance and focus on how his fingers are dancing around where I want him to be. "If you want more, all you have to do is ask."

Goddamn, he's full of himself, but he's right.

I do want more.

I want it all.

"Well, if you're not going to ask, I'm going to take what I want," he calmly states when I remain silent.

He slips his fingers into the waistband of my underwear, humming low when he feels me hot and ready. "Your body is so responsive. Are you this way with everyone?" He glides his finger along my opening, my arousal the perfect lubricant.

"Y-yes," I stammer, biting my lip to smother my moan.

This is a total lie, and he knows it.

"I think that you're lying. I think that you've never been this turned on in your entire life. I also think you've starved this beautiful body of pleasure for too long."

Writhing against his hand, I silently beg him to put me out of my misery.

And he does.

The moment he slips his finger into me, I cry out in desperate need.

"I've never heard a sweeter song, Bluebird. It sings innocence." He then begins playing my body like a true maestro, and before long, I'm bucking against his hand, begging for a release.

"Please…"

He senses my embarrassment. "Don't ever be ashamed of this incredible body. You must know that you're absolutely stunning."

"No." I'm not fishing for compliments. I've never thought myself to be beautiful or anything special.

He tsks me. "All this long, luscious brown hair, innocent hazel eyes, full 'come fuck me' pink lips, and a body to die for. You're every man's wet dream come true."

He slips in another finger, and I gasp, as I've never felt so full. "Whoever had your body before me should be ashamed. What a complete and utter amateur. A dickless fool," he spits with bite. "They've skimmed around the surface and neglected all the good bits."

And by good bits, he means my clit.

While working his fingers deeper and deeper into me, he rubs over my center with his thumb and bites over my galloping pulse. The action is my undoing, and I come with an ear-splitting scream. My body goes totally slack, and if not for his firm fingers around my waist, I would have tumbled to the floor.

Stars flash before my closed eyes, and my heart is clawing at my chest. I'm convinced I'm going to die because I've never come this quickly and powerfully before.

"That was beautiful," he says a moment later, his breath warm on my neck.

Now that I'm not lost under his spell, I become aware of the enormous erection poking into my ass. But I can also feel the frantic beating of his heart against my back. What a visual oxymoron. Could it be he's just as affected by me as I am by him?

The thought gives me a surge of confidence. "Are you going to... fuck... me now?"

I'm frightened because I've only ever been intimate with Scott, and feeling Tiger's impressive length, I know I was dealing with half a sub, but now, I got the foot long.

Tiger chuckles low, the sound reawakening my hungry body. "Is that what you'd like?"

"Yes. Please," I shamelessly answer.

"I thought you said that you shouldn't be here. That this isn't you," he arrogantly teases in a whisper as he leads us over to the sofa. I'm engulfed by his domineering height and frame. "But I think this *is* you. You just don't know it yet."

Just as I'm about to sit down, he stops me. "Bend forward."

I hesitate for a split second before bending forward awkwardly. I place my hands on the sofa's arm, shoulder-width apart. I nervously curve my back so my ass sits high in the air. I don't even know if this is the correct positioning.

Tiger hums. "So innocent."

My uneven breath gets caught in my throat when he yanks up my dress, exposing my ass. He rubs over my behind, his touch singeing my covered flesh. Suddenly, with an unforeseen, quick tug, my underwear is ripped clean off. Granted, they were flimsy, but still, I only thought that happened in the movies.

But all thoughts of my ruined underwear are long forgotten when Tiger's belt buckle hits the floor. "Sorry, but the offensive thing was in my way, and I'm an impatient man."

A second later, I hear the unmistakable sound of a foil wrapper being torn open. "Spread those gorgeous, long legs and lean forward."

I do as he asks, wishing I had taken off my stilettos before we started.

"That's it. Beautiful," he commends before I feel him rest a hand on my hip.

My entire body is on fire, and strangely, I don't feel timid being this exposed, this vulnerable to him. He coaxes my legs farther apart, secures his hold around my waist and then drives into me with force so great, I have no other choice but to surrender to the most delicious pleasure I've ever experienced.

He's rough and instantly pumps into me, not slowing down to allow my inexperienced muscles to accept his girth. But it's exactly what I want.

"Oh... fuck, you feel incredible. I was right," he hisses between staggered breaths. "Utter amateur."

I blush as the way my body is stretching with a delicious, unfamiliar pain, I feel like this is in fact my first time.

I obviously do feel incredible, because within seconds, he's sinking into me so quickly, his vicious strokes send me crumbling forward, and I fall onto my front. I'm awkwardly draped over the arm of the sofa, my face pressed into the cushions, but Tiger keeps up his fierce rhythm, never missing a beat.

I stretch my arms out in front of me and raise my hips, taking everything he gives. Tiger growls and pulls out before swiftly sinking back into me. The action hits me in just the right way, and I cry out, needing more.

"Okay?" he breathlessly pants.

I nod in response.

He surprises me as he unfastens my hair clip and wraps the long strands of hair around his hand. He then pulls hard, resulting in my neck jarring backward. I brace myself up on my arms and lean my head back as he uses my hair as reins.

An unfamiliar knot builds in my belly, and with each stroke, each thrust, the knot gets bigger and bigger. I squeeze my inner muscles, sucking him deeper into me, never wanting to let go.

"Holy shit! Again," he commands, his breath warm on my nape, and I do.

He roars, slamming harder into me. "So *now* do you believe this is you?" he asks, referring to my earlier denial of not being able to have a one-night stand.

I don't know how he knows, but I have a sneaking suspicion I'm only able to achieve this type of satisfaction because I'm with him.

"Yes," I whimper, squeezing my eyes shut.

"I win," he proudly declares, but little does he know, I've already won.

My explosion is tethering close to the edge, but when he sweeps his hand underneath my belly and pushes my hips backward so he's driving into me harder, faster, and deeper, I detonate in a way I never thought possible. A second later, he cries out his release. His movements jarred as he milks out the last of his orgasm.

When his tight grip loosens, I flop forward, not caring that my dress is still hitched up around my waist. I'm breathless, sticky, and totally spent, but my body purrs in complete satisfaction. I just had two mind-blowing orgasms with a stranger, and who would have thought, I don't feel a lick of shame.

"Flip over," Tiger breathlessly demands, his voice heavy and raw.

"Why?" I'm almost too afraid to ask.

He gently rubs over my ass, giving it an unexpected light spank. "Because, Bluebird, I want to see if you taste as sweet as you feel."

My entire body hurts, but it hurts *so good*.

I sit up in the king-size bed, surprised that I'm actually *in* bed because the last thing I remember, I was on the sofa, yanking on Tiger's mane while he managed to make me forget my own name. Looking down, I see that I'm naked. I don't remember undressing either. Tiger must have put me to bed because I'm quite certain I passed out after orgasm number four.

"Um, hello?" I call out, shamefully realizing I don't even know Tiger's name.

I'm greeted with silence.

Turning to look at the clock on the bedside table, I see a folded note leaning against a tall glass of juice. I reach for both. Taking a sip, I open the letter, hoping it'll reveal just who my stranger is.

Thank you for a most interesting evening, Bluebird.

That's it?

I turn the note over, just in case there's more. There's not.

So, this is what a one-night stand feels like. As I look around the empty room, a room that will have to be sterilized and baptized, I don't understand what all the fuss is about. Do women really enjoy being treated like a life-size, blow-up doll?

However, I decide to ignore the sensible Baylee because she's being a Debbie Downer.

Finishing my juice, I wrap the sheet around me and go in search of my clothes. My legs ache the moment I stand, but the pain is a delicious reminder of last night's vigorous activities. I raise an interested eyebrow when I see a random white bag sitting on a velvet settee.

Waddling over, I open it up to see a pair of Chucks, a pair of jeans, a fitted knitted sweater, and a gorgeous blue silk underwear set. The color reminds me of my unusual nickname, and I can't help but wonder why Bluebird. Maybe if I stopped being a McSlutty Slut for five seconds, I could have asked him. But as

I look around the room, I know that'll never happen because he's gone.

I sigh deeply as I suddenly have the one-night stand blues.

Not that she'll help, as I know she'll congratulate me and ask for the gory details, but I need to speak to Hannah. And besides, I did leave without telling her I was going upstairs with a complete stranger.

My purse is sitting on the dresser. I hunt through it and find my phone. I see I have an abundant amount of messages, missed calls and voice mails—they're all from Hannah.

I quickly call her, awaiting a lecture from hell.

"Where have you been?"

I cringe. "Hi, Han."

"Don't 'hi Han' me! I was seconds away from calling the police. You've been gone all night. Start talking."

"Well..." I start but pause, as I don't know what the proper lead in is for a conversation such as this one. But I don't need one.

"Oh... my... god," she exclaims, drawing out each word. "You totally got laid last night!"

"Well..." I repeat, dragging my big toe along the soft carpet.

"I want to know every single detail."

I chuckle. How did I know our conversation would lead this way? "I can't right now."

"You're still there?" she admonishes.

"Yes," I squeak, looking around the room.

"Leave right now!" she commands. "A one-night stand is just that. It's a one-time-only deal. You hang around and he's going to think you're scribbling his name in love hearts all over the room."

"Well, that's not going to be a problem because I don't even know what his name is," I foolishly bite back.

Hannah gasps while I cover my face with my hand. "Just say it. I'm the world's biggest slut."

Hannah's laugh floats across the room. "Actually, I was going to say you're one lucky girl. Looks like my lectures have finally paid off. So... how was he?"

"Han," I groan. "I don't want to talk about it."

"Too bad. Meet me at Andrew's Place in an hour." Before I have a chance to object, the line goes dead.

So typical of Hannah—she always has to have the last word.

"So, tell me everything. And I mean *everything*." She stresses her point by waggling her fair eyebrows up and down.

"There's not much to tell," I lie, my cheeks revealing my dishonesty.

"Oh, bullshit. You're redder than that hickie on your neck."

My hand flies to my throat while Hannah laughs. "Baylee, you're twenty-six, not fourteen. You don't have to hide your hickies. Wear 'em with pride."

"Yeah, I do," I argue, sinking low in my seat. "This just shows the world that I allowed some stranger man to chew on my neck while he had his hands down my pants."

I don't realize I'm shouting until the lady next to us slaps her gaping husband's arm. "Oh my god, Hannah, is this normal?" I thankfully whisper this time, much to the dismay of my male audience.

"What is?" she casually asks, salting her eggs.

"This feeling of... I don't know... shame, embarrassment... wanting to do it all over again," I shyly add.

Hannah looks up at me in awe. "He was *that* good?"

"Yes, he really was. I didn't even know I could... you know," I say, using my hands to fill in the blanks.

"What?" She cocks a brow.

"Come," I whisper behind my hand. "That many times."

"How many times?" she asks, pursing her lips.

I avert my eyes. "Four."

"Four!" This time, it's her turn to yell.

"Yes," I reply with a faraway smile. "It was amazing. *He* was amazing. So different to Scott."

"And that's a good thing, right?"

I meet her curious gaze. "Totally. But he was kind of rough. And he liked to talk dirty," I confess, blushing all over again.

Hannah grins. "I never thought you'd be into the kinky stuff."

Shaking my head, I explain, "No, not like that. It was like he couldn't wait to get into my pants."

"That's hot." Hannah fans herself while I nod. "Was he a good kisser?"

I bite my lip, ashamed. "I don't know. We didn't kiss. We didn't even fully get undressed. I mean, he only saw my bottom half."

Hannah's eyes widen. "Wow, he really couldn't wait."

"He was an arrogant, cocky jerk. But he was also gentle in his own way. He called me Bluebird," I confess, reaching for my coffee.

Hannah mulls over what I just said. "So, you kind of hated him, but secretly, you loved what he was doing to you?"

I nod, burying my shame behind my cup as I take a sip.

"Sounds like a match made in heaven. Why Bluebird?" She scrunches up her nose.

I shrug, as I have been thinking the same thing. "No clue."

"So this mystery man, whose name you don't know, fucked you silly, gave you four mind-blowing orgasms, bought you new clothes..." She gestures down my torso. "And then did a runner?"

"Yup." I nod, frowning.

"Well, I'll give it to you. That's the strangest one-night stand. Ever. Who buys someone clothes?" She thinks about it for a moment before drowning her pancakes in syrup.

I clear my throat, feeling the need to defend him. "He did owe me underwear."

Hannah stops midchew. "Why?"

"Because he kind of, well, he ripped mine off."

Hannah's fork bounces off the table and onto the floor. The waitress ignores us, familiar with Hannah's theatrics. "I take it back. That's not strange, that's fucking hot."

She has no idea

"I wish I asked for his name."

Hannah steals my fork and waves it in veto. "It's best not to get hung up on personal details, Baylee. That's what one-night stands are all about. Anonymity."

I groan, dropping my head in humiliation. "I don't think it's in my genetic makeup to do that. I can't stop thinking about him."

"You can't stop thinking about his junk, you mean," she corrects around a mouthful of food.

"Maybe. I don't know," I quickly amend. "I've never been attracted to anyone that way before. And I don't even know his name. He forever will be known as Tiger, the man who rocked my world."

Hannah chokes on her juice. "Tiger?"

"Yes, 'cause of your earlier reference of grabbing the tiger by his..."

"Balls." She fills in the blanks with a grin.

"Yes."

"And did you?"

I blush, wishing I had a better poker face. "No. He was in total control," I confess, feeling foolish. "It was actually quite pathetic on my behalf."

Hannah scoffs in defiance. "A man wanting to dominate you in the bedroom is not pathetic. It's hot. His alpha dog is probably high-fiving his dick."

I shake my head, smirking. "Your crudeness never ceases to amaze me."

She laughs her magical cackle. "This is all part of moving on. You've had the perfect rebound lay, and tomorrow, you start a new chapter in your life. Life is good. Stop moping." She reaches across the table to soothe out my frown lines.

I can't help but chuckle. "I know you're right. You're totally right. I mean, no point pining over a guy I'll never see again. Right?"

"Absolutely. Besides, you'll be so busy dealing with the fox, your tiger will be long forgotten."

Chapter Two

"Han, are you sure I look okay?"

"Baylee, for the tenth time, yes, you look beautiful."

"Beautiful? I want to look professional, not beautiful." I flip down the visor to look at my reflection once again.

"Well, you look both," Hannah says, zipping in and out of morning traffic.

"Are you sure this dress isn't too much?" I ask, straightening out the gray tunic I borrowed from her wardrobe.

"Nope, it's perfect."

"And my hair?" I ask, touching my high bun.

"Perfect."

"What about my makeup?" I cringe when I examine my coral-painted lips and smoky black eyes in the visor's mirror. "This is a lot more makeup than I'm used to wearing."

Hannah laughs. "Good. You're now working for one of the most successful businessmen in the United States. You have to look the part."

"Great," I grumble, flipping up the visor. "I have to look the part of a stuck-up, corporate snob. That's not me."

"It is now," she sweetly says, making a left turn toward a private underground parking garage.

"Wow," I gasp, looking out the windshield at the soaring building in front of me. "*This* is where you work?"

"This is where we *both* work," she corrects, swiping us through the boom gates and looking for a parking space.

Placing my hands on my gurgling stomach, I groan when she kills the engine. "I feel sick, Han. I should have done more research on him."

"You'll be fine. Just don't upset the boss, cardinal rule number one." She cheerfully reaches for her blazer and leather bag from the back seat while I drag myself out of the car.

As we stroll to the elevator, our heels clicking along the concrete, I gripe, "I don't even know what he looks like."

"At least you know his name," she teases as she pushes the call button.

I nervously cover my throat and blush a deep red.

Hannah winks. "Don't worry. Makeup works magic. No one will ever know what you got up to this weekend."

I let out an exaggerated sigh. "Good, because I'd hate for my boss to know that I slept with a random stranger the night of his charity event."

"Tramp," Hannah playfully whispers behind her hand.

However, talks of my promiscuous weekend are put on hold when we're joined by a dozen or so fellow coworkers who step into the elevator with us.

When the elevator doors open and I feast my eyes on Fox Technologies. Hannah nudges me out as I'm in awe of the impressive sight before me. We march down the long carpeted hallway in silence, my gaze darting around the bright open spaces, taking in everything around me.

The walls are painted a warm cream, with beige carpeting and partitioned desks as far as the eye can see. Everyone is so ridiculously quiet, I feel like I need to whisper, not wanting to disturb the peace.

"Wow."

I walk with my head held high, trying not to squirm when I feel everyone watching me, no doubt wondering who the new meat is. Maybe if I hadn't engaged in hot AF sex, I would have met everyone. Glancing down at my black heels, I curse when I see they're scuffed.

"Okay, this is you," Hannah says once we arrive at a glass door. *Dylan Fox* is written in a frosted, elegant font, not that anyone would mistake whose lavish office this was.

I gulp.

"You'll be fine, Baylee. I'm just down the hall if you need me." She points down the corridor.

"I can do this," I affirm, taking a deep breath.

"You can." She places her hands on my shoulders. "Just remember, yes, sir, no, sir, three bags full, sir."

"I'm going to hurl." I pat over my stomach, making a pained face.

My cries fall on deaf ears as Hannah turns me and pushes me to the door. "See you at lunch."

I nod and take another breath before stepping inside the very polished looking office. The reception area is decorated in a stark, sterile white, and I'm almost certain I can see my under-wear reflecting off the polished floor.

Three black leather chairs press up against the elongated wall, a glass coffee table with boring business magazines neatly stacked atop it sits a few feet away, and a crystal vase positioned in an inlet along the far wall are the only things this boring office encompasses.

A pretty brunette sits behind an enormous counter and

smiles the moment I ungracefully enter. The desk wall she's behind has the words *AUDENTES FORTUNA LUVAT* carved into the marble. I have no idea what that means.

"May I help you?"

"H-hi." I clear my throat, as I sound as nervous as I feel. "I'm Baylee Young. I'm here to see—"

"Take a seat, Ms. Young. Mr. Fox is just on a business call. He won't be long," she says, cutting me off.

"Oh, right. Thanks." Nervously walking over to the leather chair, I take a seat, tucking my skirt beneath me. The act alerts me to the fact that I have a ladder in my stockings. "Great," I mumble under my breath.

The immaculate-looking receptionist glances at me. I smile awkwardly, while subtly pulling up my pantyhose.

I was stupid to think I could ever pull this off. Even though my last boss turned out to be a home-wrecking whore, I never felt I needed to impress her like I do Mr. Fox. His reputation for being meticulous, controlled, and anal retentive are all the things I am not.

I'm starting to second-guess myself because if he's as big an asshole as they say he is, then I know I'll find it hard to hold my tongue.

The loud intercom buzzes, jarring me from my thoughts. "You can go through now," the brunette says, gesturing to a grand door to her left.

"Thanks." Standing, I straighten out my dress. I walk over to the daunting brown door, looking at it like it's my doom.

My affirmation of 'you are *not* a coward' kicks in, and when my bravery from the weekend sweeps over me, I know I've got this. If I can have sex with a nameless stranger, then I sure as hell can do this.

Pushing open the door, I amble in with a staged confidence, hoping my act will be believed. However, that confidence turns to doggy doo when I stop dead in my tracks, almost tripping over my shoes.

No. No fucking way.

I'm greeted by the broad back of Mr. Dylan Fox. He's looking out the window, appearing lost in thought, but I know he's very much alert.

"Ms. Young." He thankfully addresses me with his back still turned because I thump on my chest, certain my heart just stopped beating.

His deep, rough voice brings back all the memories of Saturday night, and I choke... on air, because standing before me is... my tiger.

However, my mysterious Tiger now has a name, and that name is Mr. Dylan Fox, a.k.a. my boss.

Fuck you, fate. Fuck you and your sick sense of humor.

"Ms. Young?" he questions when I stand frozen and mute.

Please don't turn around. For the love of god, *please* don't turn around. This will only work if you don't turn around —ever.

But he does turn around, and when he does, I know I'm right royally screwed.

"Blue—" But he stops, regaining his slipped composure. Something I sense doesn't happen often. "Ms. Young?" he asks, raising a dark, groomed brow.

Oh no, he thinks I'm a stalker. He thinks I have gone all *Fatal Attraction* and his bunny is seconds away from being boiled alive.

"Hi." I hold up my hand and wave, cringing a second later.

"Hello," he curtly replies, placing his hands into his pressed slacks pockets.

We stand, openly staring at one another, and I'm almost certain he can see the beads of sweat collecting on my brow. He appears completely unaffected while I'm seconds away from passing out.

"Please, take a seat," he finally says, pointing to a chair.

I nod, grateful to be sitting, as I don't trust my legs.

I nervously watch as he unbuttons his suit jacket before taking a seat. He looks commanding behind his huge desk, and I can't help but remember just how commanding he can be. My cheeks instantly flush, and I lower my eyes before he reads my thoughts.

So how does one do this? How do we address the big, fat, sweaty elephant in the room?

We don't. "Your credentials are very impressive, Ms. Young. I have no doubt you'll be able to keep up with my needs."

I lick my lower lip nervously before finally looking up at him. I see he is perusing over my resume, avoiding eye contact. "Thank you, Mr. Fox," I reply, feeling beyond weird calling him by his name. "I'll try my best."

He lifts those intense eyes, his gaze lingering on my mouth. "I have no doubt that you will."

I press my thighs together. This is too much.

"You'll need this," he says after a moment of uncomfortable silence.

Opening his drawer, he produces a cell phone. He slides it along his desk, and I reach for it, careful not to make contact with his fingers.

"This is so I can reach you day or night. I expect you to be available to me twenty-four seven," he firmly explains.

I refrain from saying, 'Yes, sir,' accompanied with a salute. I instead nod. "Of course. I'll ensure I have it on me always."

He steeples his long fingers in front of him. "Very good." And then... there is silence once again.

I still can't believe he's not going to acknowledge our

encounter. His detachment ticks me off because how can he be so calm while I'm burning up inside?

Those acute eyes make me once again feel like I'm naked, and I anxiously tug at the pearls around my neck. Mr. Fox watches the movement, shifting subtly in his seat.

I don't know how I'm going to do this because right now, all I can focus on is how he feasted on my body like a starved man. My cheeks redden, giving away my thoughts. "Will that be all, Mr. Fox?" I ask, unable to sit here a second longer.

"For now, Ms. Young." His brief response irritates me further.

But I stand quickly, giving him a brisk nod. "Where would you like me to start?"

He swivels in his chair and begins typing on his laptop. "You can start by getting me a coffee. Black. No sugar."

I glare daggers at him. It's one thing to not acknowledge who I am. But it's another to treat me like a slave. Goes without saying, I see red.

"I'm not getting any younger," he mocks, his head buried in his computer, not even showing me the respect of looking at me.

That pompous... dick.

I grind down on my jawbone. "Right away, *sir*," I sarcastically quip, hoping to get a rise out of him.

I'm greeted with silence.

"I got your SOS text," Hannah says as I'm frantically pacing the bathroom, biting my nails. "Please stop moving. You're making me seasick. What's going on, Baylee?"

But I can't stop moving because the moment I do, the seriousness of my current situation will sink in and I'll be sick. "I've done a bad, bad thing, Han. Like really bad."

Hannah looks at me like I've lost my mind. "That's impossible. You've been here for"—she looks at her watch—"five minutes."

"I... shit!" I curse, running a trembling hand down my face.

"C'mon, just tell me. It can't be that bad," she states, hand on hip as she watches me continue to pace.

I spin around, spreading my hands out wide. "It's worse than bad. It's a disaster."

She waits for me to elaborate.

"I...Tiger."

Her eyes glow in mischief. "Oh my god! He tracked you down?" she says, nodding, thinking that's the reason for my insanity.

"Well, er, kind of." I rub the back of my neck.

"Kind of?" She scrunches up her face, confused by my incoherency.

"I-I-I." Blowing out a deep breath, I stop pacing and brace my hands on the basin. Lowering my head, I finally confess, "Tiger is... is..."

But the words get stuck in my throat.

"Is who?" she shrieks.

"Is... Mr. Fox," I whisper into the sink, hoping she didn't hear me.

But she does. "*Excuse me*?"

I sigh as I stare into the bowl, wishing I could escape down the drain. "My hot, multi-orgasm giver, ultimate one-night stander, is none other than my boss, Mr. Dylan Fox."

There, I said it. And it felt as shitty as I knew it would.

Silence.

"Han?" I ask a second later, hesitantly turning to look at her.

Her mouth is wide open, and her eyes are bulging from her head. "You're not serious?"

"I so am."

Hannah shakes her head, and her surprise suddenly transforms to humor. "Sweet baby Jesus, this is a..."

"A nightmare." I fill in the blanks.

"Hilarious," she settles for instead.

It's now my turn to look at her like she's the deranged one. "Hilarious? Have you not heard a word I said?"

"I heard, and this is funny."

I raise both eyebrows, not seeing how she could possibly find my predicament funny.

"C'mon, you've gotta see the funny side to this. I mean, what are the odds you finally have the balls to have a one-night stand, and it's with your boss!"

I rub my brow. "I didn't know he was my boss at the time."

"And that's what makes this even funnier." And she bursts into fits of laughter.

"You're quite possibly the world's worst friend." I splash some water on my face while Hannah continues cackling at my expense.

"I have to quit. I can't work here," I utter, watching Hannah wipe the tears from her eyes.

"Don't be silly. Of course you can. How'd he act?"

"Purely professional," I confess, even though his professionalism pissed me off.

"And how'd you act?"

"Like a raving lunatic."

Hannah bites her lip to contain her laugh. "Did he acknowledge you?"

"No."

Hannah flinches. "Well, that's a little awkward."

"Try a lot," I groan, massaging my temple.

"Baylee, stop." She grips both my upper arms, shaking some sense into me. "You're good at your job. You can do this with your eyes closed. It's probably better that you do," she adds, pulling an amused face.

I ignore her joke. "How am I meant to do this? I mean, this is so wrong. If anyone ever found out…"

"They won't." She stops me from continuing by giving me a light shake. "There is no way he'd tell anyone. And I know you'd rather die. So I dare say your secret is safe."

"That's the problem. I don't want to have a secret. Nor do I want to be a secret. I just want to come in, do my job, and go home. My life has been complicated enough. I don't need this to add to the ever-growing shit pile."

She pulls a sympathetic face. "You kind of don't have a choice. If you want to keep working here, then you'll have to suck it up and forget you ever met anyone you nicknamed Tiger because that man out there"—she points to the door—"is not him."

I nod because she's right. And that's what blows.

Thankfully, I haven't seen Tiger, I mean, Mr. Fox since this morning. He's been in meetings all day and left me to learn the ropes from Alicia, the brunette receptionist.

"He likes his coffee served at precisely eight-oh-two a.m. Not a second later. And he prefers meetings with clients to take place after eight-thirty a.m."

I nod, chewing the top of my pencil as I slouch in my seat, bored out of my brain.

She looks at my blank notepad. "You should write that down."

"Oh right," I say, sitting upright, but seriously, how hard can this be?

I worked for the soulless whore for three years, and not once did I need to take notes or be briefed on what brand pen she preferred. Working for Mr. Fox, our history aside, is definitely going to be a challenge.

"Ms. Pope. Ms. Young," Mr. Fox addresses us as he briskly marches into reception.

Alicia shoots up while I slouch back down in my seat, ignoring how his deep voice triggers my heart to race. I doodle in my notepad, pretending to be lost in my ever so interesting lesson of, 'how to please your anal retentive boss.'

"How'd she go?" he asks, shuffling through the documents Alicia presents to him.

"Great, sir. She'll be ready in no time."

She?

She is the cat's mother, and not to mention, I'm sitting right here. His continued aloofness once again pisses me off so I raise my eyes, daring him to call me *she* again. He meets my challenge and the corner of his mouth curves into a bold smile. It's gone a second later.

He returns his attention to the perfect Alicia. "Excellent. Have her look over the Fletcher notes. I need them typed up by the end of the day."

"Of course, sir."

He completely ignores me, and just as I'm about to stand and give this jerk a piece of my mind, he slams his office door shut, ending a conversation that never started.

My mouth hinges open. That was unexpected, not to mention rude. I can't help but wonder if this is the reason why he's gone through so many assistants. Or am I just the lucky one?

I decide to ask. "So," I say as Alicia sits back down. "How long have you worked for Mr. Fox?"

She brushes her long hair to one shoulder. "Oh, I don't work for him. I fill in when he's in need of assistance."

"I'm guessing that's a common occurrence then by how well you know the job."

She nervously shuffles her paperwork, avoiding my gaze and questions. But I won't allow her code of silence to deter me. "C'mon, you can tell me."

Alicia shakes her head, her lips pulled into a thin line.

"I promise," I declare, holding my hand up in oath. "My lips are sealed."

Just as I think she's come around, a sharp voice rains on my parade. "Ms. Young, a word. Now."

I instantly drop my hand, guiltily looking at the doorway of Mr. Fox's office. Judging by the pissy look on his face, he no doubt heard me begging for dirt.

Alicia quickly busies herself, ensuring he knows she wasn't an accomplice—traitor.

"Fine." I sigh, throwing my pen in defiance and standing lacklusterly.

The moment I walk over to him, our eyes lock. However, I don't allow his bully tactics to scare me. I push past him when he doesn't budge an inch and tell my disloyal body to stop with the celebrating when we touch.

The door closes behind me, and I stand before his desk, refusing to sit and be reprimanded like a naughty school child. My back is turned to him, but I can feel his glare, and once again, I feel like prey. But I stand tall and pull my shoulders back because if he wants to pretend, then so can I.

"How's your first day going so far, Ms. Young?"

"Fine, Mr. Fox." I swallow deeply when I hear his footsteps pad softly on the carpet.

"And you're finding everyone to be well-mannered and helpful?"

"Yes."

"That's good to hear."

When I feel him come to a stop inches from my back, my body begins to tremble. "I would appreciate it then if you could show the same respect. I don't tolerate cattiness in my office, so if you have a question, I would prefer you ask me rather than badger my staff."

So he did hear me. Is he spying on me now? Shouldn't surprise me seeing as he's a complete control freak. A trait I thoroughly enjoyed in the bedroom, but now, it just ticks me off.

"Yes, sir." The defiance can be heard in my tone.

"Ms. Young, this relationship can go one of two ways."

I remain quiet, indicating I'm listening.

"My way, or no way. You'll soon see my way is the best for the both of us."

I bite my cheek as I'm seconds away from telling him his way can suck it.

"We clear?"

"Crystal," I grit out from between clenched teeth.

"Good. Now seeing as you think there's time to socialize, I'll send Ms. Pope home and you can proceed on your own."

That bastard. I'm going to drown on my own, but I'll be damned if I admit that to him. "Whatever you wish, sir."

When he takes a step closer, I can feel his warmth against my back. It reminds me of Saturday night.

"I wish for you to—" But he pauses, his labored breathing buttering my flesh in a fine sheet of goose bumps.

But I stand rigid, still refusing to show him I'm affected by his presence. The room is suddenly filled with a heated static, and I focus on what's important—like breathing.

"Have Ms. Pope show you the files I require for this afternoon's presentation," he instructs, not completing his original thought.

I nod, afraid if I speak, he'll hear how breathless I sound.

"That'll be all," he says, dismissing me.

Internally counting to three, I slowly turn, very aware that he still hasn't moved. When I meet him face first, those breaths leave me gasping for more. No matter his arrogance, I can't deny I'm so attracted to him it hurts.

What is the matter with me? Am I really that fucked up?

Has Scott's infidelity short-circuited my good sense because the old me would never find someone this egotistical attractive? But maybe that's the problem. Maybe the old me was a boring stick-in-the-mud who needed to lighten up.

Either way, that person is long gone because this is new the Baylee—2.0. And this new Baylee doesn't take shit from anyone —her hot, incredibly sexy new boss included.

I stand my ground, ensuring my body doesn't betray me when he continues standing in front of me, his enormous frame blocking my exit. "Is there anything else, sir?" I ask when he makes no attempt to move.

I make no secret that every time I address him as 'sir,' I'm internally flipping him off.

His mouth twitches, and it's gestures such as these that confuse me. One minute he's Satan reincarnate, and the next, for a split second, he's human. The human who made my body hum like no one was ever able to before.

He steps out of my way.

I try not to be too obvious as I practically run for the safety of the exit. Just as I'm about to yank open the door, his hoarse voice stops me in my tracks. "By the way, Ms. Young, I like your shoes."

Peering down, I see the shoes in question are the ones I

wore Saturday night. The same ones I wore when he was fucking me over the arm of the sofa. The same shoes that were digging into his back, drawing him closer as he was nestled between my thighs.

Touché Tiger, you may have won this round, but you've just shown me that you're human after all.

I'm surrounded by mountains upon mountains of paperwork with no end in sight.

The entire day was an utter disaster, as I had no idea what I was doing. But I'd rather cut out my own tongue than ask Mr. Asshole for help.

His comment about my shoes revealed that he too, at some point, had thought about our meeting. Maybe his tough exterior was his way of coping with an awkward situation? Or maybe he's just a sociopathic jerk?

I'm betting on the latter option.

Sighing, I look around my cluttered desk, seeing no end in sight any time soon.

"Hey, pretty lady. You ready to go home?"

"Ha! That's not going to happen in this millennium," I quip, looking at Hannah over my tower of paperwork.

"He expects you to do all of this by tonight?" She sweeps her hand out over my desk incredulously.

Looking at the clock on my computer, I pop my gum calmly. "Actually, he expected this on his desk by five. So it's actually an hour and two minutes late."

"He surely can't expect you to get all of this done. I mean, today is your first day."

I sarcastically laugh. "Tell that to The Antichrist."

She shakes her head. "No thanks. I like my job. I thought he'd go easy on you because—"

And she raises her eyebrows.

My finger flies up to cover my lips. "Shh. These walls have ears."

She laughs. "Okay, well, call me when you're done, and I can come pick you up."

"It's okay, Han. I'll be here all night. I'll just catch a cab or train."

"Are you sure?"

"Positive. Go enjoy your sofa."

"Okay, love you. Don't work too hard," she teases over her shoulder.

I chuckle to myself. "Too late for that."

Adding the final touches to a document, I press print and sigh in relief. My tired muscles groan in protest when I stand and make my way over to the printer. A yawn escapes me as I wait for the two-hundred-page document to print.

What a day. As much as it sucked, I love being back in the workforce.

Before my boss turned into a betraying she-devil, I loved working for her. I thrived on the deadlines, and enjoyed delivering before they were due. I guess I'm an overachiever. I always have been.

Although Dylan is a major pain in the ass, a small part of me is grateful he took a chance on someone he never met unknowingly before Saturday night. But I'd sooner eat glass than tell him that.

"Are you still here, Ms. Young?"

"Sweet mother of god!" I yelp, pressing a hand to my chest. Lost in thought, I failed to hear Mr. Fox exit his office. "Don't you know it's rude to sneak up on people," I admonish, spinning around.

"I was hardly sneaking," he replies with a lopsided smirk. Goddamn, he's handsome when he's not a sourpussed jerk.

"Regardless, make some noise next time," I bark, ignoring his smile.

"Noted. I'll be sure to announce my arrival next time." Is he making a joke?

Again, I ignore him because I can't deal with his mood swings.

"Good."

We stand staring at one another, that familiar static once again crackling between us. I wish it would stop because it's giving me whiplash. Everything about Mr. Dylan Fox gives me whiplash.

"These files will be on your desk in five minutes. Sorry, they're late," I apologize, needing to fill the silence.

He nods.

"And the transcripts for today's meeting will be on your desk by the morning." I leave out the fact I'll be here all night finishing it.

"Excellent."

Silence once again.

These pauses are making me edgy, so I turn around, busying myself with the copier.

"Well," he says with pause. "Good night then."

"Good night."

Why is he still here?

I hold my breath, only letting it out when I hear the elevator ding.

What is it about this man? I'm pretty sure I hate him, but why do I want to tear his clothes off every time I'm in the same room as him. "Because you're crazy, Baylee," I mumble to myself, running a hand down my face.

Once the copier spits out the final page, I bind it and make my way into Dylan's office. Once inside, I tell myself in and out, as it's totally unprofessional snooping around in your boss's belongings. But so is sleeping with the boss. And besides, I've broken all the rules. What's one more?

I casually place the files on his desk, peering around his generous, orderly office. This is the office of a control freak, where every little thing has a place and purpose—how entirely boring and drab.

Unable to help myself, I take a tour, ensuring not to touch anything along the way. There are no personal belongings in here. No picture frames, no trophies, no awards, nothing to give me a better idea of who my boss is. Maybe that's what he wants. This is his place of business. He obviously conducts his matters of pleasures in hotel rooms with complete strangers.

The huge bay window reveals breathtaking views of Boston and the Marina. I can imagine Tiger sitting in his high-backed leather chair, staring out the window, thinking about work, money, and the women he's screwed. I wonder if he's thought about me. It's only fair, seeing as I can't seem to stop thinking about him.

Pulling out his seat, I feel like an utter rebel as I slouch into his chair. The leather feels soft yet hard underneath my body, and I can't help but compare it to that of its owner. Spinning it around, I lean backward and take in the views before me. It's quite peaceful being alone this high up.

My mind wanders to thoughts of Scott. I wonder what he's doing and if he's happy. A part of me hopes that he isn't. He ruined my life,, and he also ruined me. But being with Tiger was the first time I felt alive in months. In a weird, twisted way, he gave me hope that maybe I'll actually be okay. He gave me the courage to be myself, while not that long ago, I didn't know who that was.

By letting go, I've never felt freer. I've never felt happier because much as I hate to admit it, Scott cheating on me didn't come as a surprise. Yes, the person he cheated on me with was a surprise, but the action itself was long overdue. We were kids when we got together, and I could see him losing interest in us every day.

Still lost in thought, I don't hear my phone chime but rather feel it vibrate against my leg. Reaching for it, I see I have a text from Mr. Fox.

> How are those files coming along?

I jolt up in my seat, almost falling onto my ass. Quickly looking from left to right, I let out a sigh of relief when I see that the coast is clear.

> Almost done.

Which is a complete lie.
He replies almost instantly.

> I'm most pleased. Ensure the Cheing file goes out first thing tomorrow morning. 7 am.

I salute at his demand, thankful he can't see me. Or can he? He responds a moment later.

> Thank you

I'm beyond paranoid being in here, as I'm afraid he'll decide to pay me an impromptu visit to ensure I'm not snooping on his personal belongings—which is exactly what I'm doing.

Carefully wheeling his chair back to where it was sitting, I rearrange the files so they're sitting perfectly straight. Taking one last look around the sterile office, which smells like the inside of a citrus cleaning spray bottle, I have an idea.

Creeping across the soft beige carpet, I stop at his bookshelf and run my finger over the spines of the alphabetically placed volumes. Tiger needs to let go and live. Being this disciplined is so boring.

Closing my eyes, I whisper under my breath, "Eeny..." Blindly running my finger along the spines of leathered books, I begin my devious scheme. "Meeny... miny..." I squiggle my finger downward and stop at a random book. "Moe."

My eyes snap open as I'm curious to see what my finger landed on. I can't help but chuckle when I see the book in question is *Moby Dick*.

Carefully pulling it out, I scan through the other various tedious titles, deciding that *Moby Dick* should be acquainted with Edward and Bella. Defiantly, I run over to my desk and riffle through my bag to find my tattered copy of *Twilight*.

Skipping back into his office, I slide the book into the place where *Moby Dick* once sat. "You need a little revolt in your perfect, organized life, *sir*." I grin, pleased with my uprising. I wonder how long it'll take for Tiger to sniff out the anarchy.

And more importantly, what he'll do once he does.

Chapter Three

The next morning, I walk into Fox Technologies nursing my tall cappuccino like it's my lifeline. It took me half the night, but I did it. I got everything Mr. Fox wanted done, and I totally aced it.

I vaguely listen to Hannah as she suggests we go out Friday night for drinks with a few coworkers. "Sure, Han, sounds fun."

She latches on to my arm while I almost trip over my heels. When she touches my forehead, I shrink away. "Quit it."

I laugh quietly, looking around the office to ensure no one saw.

"Sorry, I was just making sure you felt okay."

"Ha, ha, very funny," I mock, stopping outside my office.

"I'll see you for lunch?"

"If I'm allowed out of my prison, then yes," I tease, half joking.

Hannah smirks. She turns to leave but stops. "Oh, nice shoes."

Looking down at my shoes, which have been dubbed "the shoes," I can't keep the banter from my tone when I reply, "They keep me on my toes."

"That they do," she responds with a wink.

I wave her goodbye and use my butt to open the door, as I have a coffee tray in one hand and my briefcase in the other.

"Well, that's one way to open a door."

I shriek, almost dropping my loot. "Jesus Christ! You need to wear a bell around your neck," I exclaim, entering the office foyer and ignoring the eagle eyes of my boss. He looks exceptional in a navy pinstripe suit, crisp white shirt, and, gasp... a blood-red tie.

"Are you suggesting I'm to wear a collar, Ms. Young?"

Shrugging, I hope I appear unaffected. "Sure, if that's your thing." I brush past him as he leans against my desk, watching my every move.

Willing my shaky fingers to stop betraying my nerves, I go about setting up, pretending he's not there. "Oh, here you go. Here is your tall blonde roast, no milk."

"Thank you." He accepts the coffee appreciatively.

However, that appreciation soon turns to annoyance when I see him lift up the cup to read the name scribbled on the front. In big red letters, the name 'Jackass' can be clearly seen.

He peers over at me, cocking a brow.

"Oh." I fake innocence, barely biting back my smile. "They must have misheard me."

He doesn't believe a word. "Indeed." He continues standing and staring at me while I fluff around my desk, unsure why he's still here.

His cologne is doing things to my hormones, and I swallow. "Is there anything else?" I ask, using my notepad as a barricade between us, as he's making it more than obvious he's currently undressing me with those striking eyes.

He cocks his head to the side. "Yes, there is. Follow me." He turns on his heel and walks into his office, leaving the door open.

Into the lion's den, I go once again.

"Shut the door," he commands when I enter. He is leaning against the edge of his desk, arms and ankles folded. He is a picture of perfection, but underneath that perfection, I can sense things are about to get messy.

I do as he asks and wait for him to speak.

"How do you like your job?" he randomly queries.

"I—" My voice gets caught in my throat. I clear my throat twice before answering. "I find it challenging, but I enjoy a challenge."

He raises a brow. "How is it challenging?"

Trying not to scoff at such a ridiculous question, I put on my best professional face. "Well, look around," I say, sweeping my hand to his office. "You like control. You demand perfection. I just hope I can deliver because I really want this job."

He nods and pushes off the desk. "Do I make you nervous, Ms. Young?" he asks as I clutch my hands behind my back.

I lie. "No, sir."

"How do I make you feel then?" He takes a step closer while I force myself to stand my ground.

I don't know in what aspect he's asking, so I answer professionally. "You make me want to be the best that I can be. I want to please you."

Those sensual lips tip into a knowing smile. "And you have."

I gulp.

Taking another step closer, he stands self-assuredly as I squirm. I hate his confidence because it turns me on. I love to hate this arrogant beast in front of me.

"What do you think of my office?"

I know there is a reason for the twenty questions, so I play along. Looking around, the only words that come to mind are wearisome, colorless, and dull, but I shrug. "It's... great."

He laughs and I jolt, startled to hear the uncommon sound. "Great. Great is such a noncommittal word, Ms. Young. What is exactly *great* about it?"

"Um..." My brows knit together. "The view?"

"The view," he repeats, appearing to be deep in thought. "I suppose you're right. The view is rather *great*. Anything else?"

I don't know what he wants me to say. He's toying with me, and I don't like it.

"There are no wrong or right answers. Just your honest opinion."

Honestly, there is nothing great about this sterile, orderly office. Personally, I like disorder. This is way too much methodical for me. So I remain quiet, deciding that's the better option than being caught out on a lie.

"Your silence reveals there is in fact nothing "great" to be found in here. Would you mind sharing what you find offensive?"

Is this another trick question? Is this a test, and if I fail, I'll be on the first bus out of here?

Deciding to be honest, I meet his confident stare. "It's just a little too controlled for me, sir. You can't even see the floor in my bedroom," I share, opting to leave out the fact my floor is the living room floor.

"Oh? So you like disorder and chaos?" His words are dripping in innuendo as he saunters around me.

"Why are you asking me this?" I ask, turning to look at him over my shoulder.

"Because, Ms. Young, I'm trying to understand why you would feel the need to bring your disorder into my office."

"My what?" I instantly look down at my clothes. Did I miss a button on my blouse?

"Obviously my office is not to your liking because you felt the need to redecorate."

"Redecorate?"

When he stops in front of his bookshelf, I get it. I can't believe he saw it already. I was expecting at least a week for him to notice and by that time, anyone could have done it. But now, I'm caught red-handed.

I lower my eyes, feeling my cheeks heat. I can see the glow reflecting off his polished Italian loafers.

I don't know why I did it. I just wanted to ruffle his perfect feathers. Just like I want to run my hand through his slicked-back hair and free his imprisoned locks. What a boring, unsatisfied life he must live, where everything has a place. I can't help but wonder where my place is. He makes it clear a moment later.

"If I wanted to redecorate, I'd hire a fucking interior designer," he barks, his jaw firm. "Do that again, and you'll be looking for another job. Understood?"

He's serious. It was meant to be a joke. But the hard look in his eye reveals Mr. Fox doesn't appreciate the humor. He *is* as anal retentive as he acts and sounds.

"I said... do you... understand?" he asks, speaking as if I'm an imbecile.

Not appreciating his tone whatsoever, I bite back, "Yes, sir."

"Good. Now go get me another coffee. One without the juvenile antics, if you could."

I stand stunned, but I don't know what I expected. The man has gone through personal assistants faster than I can say 'Fuck you, Mr. Dylan Fox, and the godlike complex you embrace!'

51

"That'll be all, Ms. Young," he says when I remain rooted to the spot.

My eyes fill with hot, angry tears, but I bite them back as I refuse to show weakness. I nod, and he turns his back to me, placing his hands in his pockets.

What a dismissal.

Walking over to his desk, I refrain from throwing the scalding coffee in his face as I snatch it off the polished surface. I hold my head up high as I walk past him. He doesn't turn, nor does he acknowledge I'm there.

Well, fuck him. I refuse to allow another man to treat me like dirt.

I take a quick peep over my shoulder to ensure his back is still turned. It is. With bated breath, I speedily reach for a hideous glass ornament of a duck, which is perched on the filing cabinet and totally out of place, as I didn't take him for a duck lover. Without delay, I turn it around and smile smugly.

I contain my laughter and exit the room.

The rest of the week is just as bad as the start, and when Friday rolls through, I welcome it with tequila and limes.

"I promise, as soon as I can afford my own place, Han, I'll be out of your hair," I assure her, tossing my dirty clothes into my makeshift hamper.

Hannah's small apartment is barely big enough for her. But that's the price she's willing to pay for an apartment with a view.

"It's fine." She waves me off, pouring us shot number three. "I like you and your messiness."

"At least someone does."

"I still can't believe you screwed with him that way, and you've still got a job." She tosses back a shot, making a pained face the moment it goes down.

When she passes me mine, I relish in the burn. "Fire me for what?" I ask, wiping my mouth with the back of my hand. "For touching his precious books? I'll sue his ass for unfair dismissal."

"He's fired people for a lot less," she reveals, leaning against the kitchen counter.

"Really?"

"Yes, which makes me believe under his tough exterior, he's all gooey soft for you."

Letting out a sarcastic laugh, I declare, "Soft? Did you not hear me when I detailed how he made me his personal slave all week?"

"Well, forget about him." She waves further talks of Mr. Fox off. "It's the weekend, baby, and we're going to not remember it."

When she holds up two shot glasses, I drop the basket and happily reach for one. "I'll drink to that." We toss back our tequila, both opening and closing our mouths in distaste.

"Okay, let's do this!" I slam my glass on the counter.

"You're not wearing that are you?" Hannah pulls a face while sucking on a lime.

"Yes, why?" I look down at my jeans, Chucks, and off-the-shoulder black tee.

"I may or may not have mentioned to Ken that you were coming tonight," she playfully reveals, but I have no idea what she's talking about.

"Who?"

"Ken," she repeats, but it's not ringing any bells. She throws in another clue. "The hottie I introduced you to at lunch yesterday."

"I have no idea who you're talking about. Did I even eat lunch yesterday?"

Hannah bursts into fits of laughter. "Yes, although you were hacking into your steak like you were envisioning it to be someone's face."

Ding! Ding! Ding!

"Oh yeah, now I remember."

"Who, Ken?"

"No, the steak," I clarify.

"C'mon, it'll be fun. Throw on that little black dress which shows off your assets," and she winks.

Rolling my eyes, I reply, "No offense, Han, but the last time I listened to you and showed off my assets, I got screwed, literally, by my boss, who just happens to be a pig. Actually, pig is a compliment, as I actually like pigs."

Hannah is holding back her smile.

"What's so funny?" I prop my hand on my hip.

"You so wanna fuck him."

I throw a lime at her. "Fuck you."

The club we're at isn't exactly the place I'd usually choose to go to, but shots are two dollars, so I'm not complaining.

Turns out, I do remember meeting Ken. I'm actually surprised I forgot because he's gorgeous. With curly brown hair, hypnotizing jade eyes, and a killer smile, he's someone most women would fall over to talk to. Not to mention he's polite and not at all cocky, but as he's talking to me about his goals and dreams, I feel my eyelids grow heavy as I smother yawn number ten behind my hand.

What is the matter with me?

Ken is exactly the type of man I should be interested in, but I'm not. That thought has me tossing back another shot.

Hannah nudges me with her knee, and I lean in close. "So, what do you think of Mr. Dreamy Eyes?"

"He's great." I bite my lip to stop my smile. *"Great is such a noncommittal word, Ms. Young."*

Ugh, get out of my head! But secretly, I like that all thoughts lead back to him.

"That goofy smile reveals you think someone else is a lot more than just great."

The loud dance music drowns out my groan. "What is the matter with me, Han? I'm messed up. He's a complete jerk, not to mention a complete control freak, but whenever I'm in his presence, I feel... alive."

Hannah doesn't reply, but I sense her bewilderment over this situation as she sips her cocktail.

"Scott was safe," I continue, needing to say this out loud. "And I felt grounded, but with Tiger"—I lower my voice so our colleagues won't hear—"I feel like I'm breaking all the rules... and I like it."

Hannah pulls back, grinning. "Who would have thought little Baylee Young is a rule breaker."

"Yes, I'm surprised, too."

"Whatever will your grandmother's parish down in Louisiana say?"

"Shh!" I giggle, placing my finger over my lips. "Jesus will hear you."

Hannah chuckles, and we guzzle back another shot. The booze has lightened me up, and this is the first time since Scott that I've felt happy.

There are about twenty fellow employees here tonight, and I'm proud that I've spoken to most. They've all asked what it's like working for Mr. Fox, and I've been as diplomatic as I can be. Consensus is everyone thinks he's an uptight asshole who needs to loosen up. But it's to be expected that a thirty-one-year-old, successful businessman would be a little neurotic.

I've tried to subtly ask what his back story is, but no one knows, as he doesn't openly share his personal life. I make it a point to investigate later.

"Are you going to dance?" Ken asks into my ear. His closeness and warmth startle me, and I pull back.

"No. I'm an awful dancer, and not to mention, I think I'm drunk." Looking at the table littered with empty shot glasses and bottles, I amend, "Actually, I don't think, I am."

"That's okay. I won't let you fall." Before I can object, he places his hand on my lower back.

With no other choice, I cast him a strained smile. "Okay. But don't say I didn't warn you."

He smirks his award-winning smile and leads me to the dance floor.

A group of us begin dancing, with Hannah in the middle, tossing her hair from side to side. An upbeat dance song plays loudly on the speakers, sending the vibrant crowd into a dancing frenzy.

I hobble awkwardly, feeling ridiculous, as I don't usually listen to Top 40. Ken must see my uncomfortableness because he subtly shuffles in front of me and begins giving me my own personal floor show. He's got the moves, and I can't deny he looks hot. So when he places a hand lightly on my hip and draws me close so we're inches apart, I don't shy away.

I'm a lot shorter than he is, so he dips low. "Having fun?"

I nod.

"I would really love to take you out one day."

Pulling back, I resist the urge to clear out my ears. "What?"

He smiles, guiding my hips to continue moving to the music. "You're not seeing anyone, are you?"

"No, I'm not..." But this is too soon. I squash down the inner voice which is screaming at me that it wasn't too soon to sleep with your boss.

"Hannah told me you broke up with your ex-boyfriend months ago." His heavy breathing gusting against my neck is suddenly making me itchy.

"I did, but..."

"But I'd really like to get to know you better. No pressure, of course." He leans in close, his lips pressing against my cheek.

I feel like I'm suffocating, and his heavy-handed cologne suddenly makes me gag. I pull away so quickly, I'm certain I've given myself whiplash. "If you'll excuse me, I have to use the restroom," I explain when he looks at me, baffled.

"Oh. I'll come with you." When he attempts to slip his hand into mine, I shrug away and out of his hold.

"It's okay. I won't be long."

He reads my brush off loud and clear, but smiles.

Pushing my way through the sweaty, gyrating bodies is quite a mission, and when I finally break through, I breathe out a sigh of relief. After the awkward PDA, I need a drink, but the bar is crammed full with a line of thirsty patrons. Not wanting to make a liar out of myself, I decide to hit the restroom and then sober up with a few gallons of water.

It's so impossibly loud in here; my ringing ears thank me when I reach the restrooms. Of course, the line is a mile long, but I happily wait as I need a breather from Ken and his getting-to-know-me speech. He's known me for all of five seconds. Why is he asking me out? His forwardness has just confirmed that I'm not interested in dating any time soon.

However, I didn't have any qualms about having sex with a complete stranger. What does that say about my morality?

My bag vibrates against my leg, so I open it up, thankful for the distraction. I search for my phone, in beliefs it's Hannah, asking where I've gone. I gag on my tongue when I see who the text message is from.

> Are you having a pleasant evening?

That single phrase sends my senses into overdrive. Why is Mr. Fox texting me?

I stare at the screen, unsure of how to respond.

> I am, thank you. I'll have the notes you requested for Monday's 9 a.m. meeting on your desk by 7:45 a.m.

I have no idea why he's texting me. I assume it's work related.

> Thank you. Where are you?

I raise an eyebrow.

> I'm out.

> Anywhere special.

> Not really.

> Such noncommittal answers. I'm disappointed, Ms. Young. Next thing you'll tell me is the place you're at is great.

I gulp.

Why is he making small talk? He's so confusing. It's like he can sense I'm trying to have a pleasant evening without him.

> I'll have you know the place, and the people I'm with are really great.

What people?

> Just people.

Stop being so vague.

> Stop being so nosy!

I press send before I talk some sense into my heated brain. Just when I think I've overstepped a line, my phone dings.

Where are you?

> You'll never find me. Have a nice weekend.

This is getting me nowhere, and he's ruining my high.

Try not to make any decisions you'll regret when sober.

Squeaking, I duck low and look around me. The girl next to me almost certainly thinks I've lost my mind.

How would he know I'm faced with a decision? And how does he know I'm drunk?

There is no way he's here, I reason. This is not his scene. And besides, it's not like he's interested in me and my movements. He's hardly spoken to me all week. I toss my phone into my bag and quickly make a beeline for the door as I need to get out of this stifling room.

The moment I push open the door, I bump straight into someone, and déjà vu hits me so hard I almost fall to the floor.

The same warm hands steady me, the same perfume assaults my brain, and the same feelings overwhelm my entire body. I feel like I'm going to explode.

Peering up, I see the impassioned indigo eyes of my Tiger. He looks incredible, and suddenly, nothing else exists but him. I trip over my tongue, not knowing what to say. But he fills in the silence by abruptly pushing me up against the wall, caging me in with his arms up by my head.

I'm dazed, surprised, and so unbelievably turned on; I don't even know what to do. Anyone can see us out here in the long open corridor, but he doesn't seem to care.

"Found you," he growls, lowering his lips to my ear. "The question is, now that I've found you, whatever should I do?"

I can think of only one thing. And so can he.

I reach for him the moment he reaches for me, and we frantically meet halfway, smashing our lips in a union of wanton desire. This kiss is not sweet, nor do we take it slow. We're all tongue and teeth, but a kiss has never been more perfect. Our first kiss is everything I thought it would be and more.

I tug at his T-shirt, desperate to feel his flesh against mine, but he reaches for my hand and slams it above my head. The dominant move drives me wild, and I thrust my chest against his. He fists his free hand into my loose hair, securing a firm grip, angling my mouth to suit his demanding tongue.

I'm enclosed in Tiger's cage, and I never want to be set free.

I'm swept away by his rough, lust-filled kisses, I can hardly breathe, but who needs air because before this kiss, I was barely living. His supple lips seal firmly over mine, his fierce tongue fucking me passionately, reminding me of the inferno his tongue left between my legs. The memory has me whimpering into his mouth, shamelessly demanding an encore. But he abruptly ends the kiss.

Pinning me with a no-nonsense stare, he states, "Talk to the Ken Doll again, and he'll be looking for a new job."

I cry out when he audaciously presses his knee against my core.

"Such sweetness, Bluebird, but yet, such fierceness too." He thumbs my trembling bottom lip.

He called me Bluebird. He does care.

The fact leaves me needy, and I swoop forward for another kiss. But he's still restraining me. I groan, which elicits a laugh from him. He is enjoying my frustration.

Not caring how desperate I sound, I gripe, "You've been mean to me all week. How about you cut me some slack?"

"Me? Mean?" He fakes shock, a trace of a grin lighting up his handsome face. "Ms. Young, I'm utterly offended."

"You're an utter pig," I retort, fruitlessly pulling from his grip.

He chuckles deeply, untroubled by my insult. "What I'd like to do to that smart mouth of yours."

"I dare you," I challenge, feeling my heart race. For once, he looks speechless. "What's wrong, *sir*? Cat got your tongue?"

"I'd rather you have it," he grunts before swooping forward and slamming his lips over mine.

I'm breathless, needy, and pretty sure my kisses are resembling a fourteen-year-old, inexperienced schoolgirl with how much tongue I'm using, but I don't care. I'm kissing the man who I've wanted to strangle all week. Even now, his bossiness is infuriating me, but I let it slide because I would rather die than stop kissing him.

As our kiss intensifies to pornographic proportions, he loosens his grip on my wrist and places my hand between us, boldly brushing over the enormous hard-on poking into me. He bites and sucks my bottom lip before pulling away.

"Let's get a hotel room."

His words douse my high and I pull away, stunned. "Excuse me?"

What's wrong with his house? I know for a fact he only lives about twenty minutes from here. So why rent a room?

Awful, horrible thoughts crash into me, and the truth of what I'm doing hits home. I'm just another Fox Fan he thinks he can use and abuse whenever his dick calls.

Well, no more.

He senses my mood shift immediately. "Bluebird—"

But it's too late.

"Don't Bluebird me." I tighten my hold on his privates.

He wheezes while I rejoice in the sound. "You are a presumptuous asshole, and I need my head checked. I don't even like you very much—actually, at all. Quite frankly, you disgust me. You're bossy, moodier than a premenstrual teen and you have the worst manners—ever! I am not one of your whores, Mr. Fox."

The moment I let his balls go, he sags in relief, but he looks angrier than a bear with a sore head.

"You want to pretend that you don't know me. Well, that suits me just fine. Forget tonight, or any other night, for that matter, happened." I'm so angry, I'm shaking.

He simply nods, the perfect poker face in place.

I was stupid to think he ever cared.

Feeling hot tears approaching, I push past him, disappointed when he doesn't attempt to stop me. "Have a nice night, Mr. Fox. I'll see you on Monday."

I turn on my heel and leave behind something that'll never be.

"Here, drink this," Hannah coos, setting a peppermint tea in front of me. "It'll help your stomach." I appreciate the thought, but tea is not going to soothe my heartache.

I'm still so freaking mad. I have no idea how I'm going to be able to go in to work on Monday without unleashing my wrath on Mr. Fox's smug face. I know this is my fault, but a small, stupid part of me romanticized that he actually liked me. But his actions last night proved otherwise.

The only person he cares about is himself and his dick! The thought gives me an idea.

"Pass over my laptop, Han."

She nods and hands it to me as she sits down on the sofa. "What are you doing?"

"I need to find out who he is. Why he is the way that he is. I need to understand why he thinks he can treat me like dirt."

"Um, because he's a prick. Sometimes, there just isn't an explanation. Just like Scott."

This time, I don't react as badly to his name being mentioned.

"I don't buy it," I stubbornly retort, powering up my computer. "I need the dirt on him. I need to know just who exactly Mr. Dylan Fox is."

"He's a womanizing jerk! I can't believe he kissed you and was all like, 'Bluebird, such sweetness.'" She lowers her voice in an attempt to sound like him, which is quite comical. "Then he's all, 'Hey bitch, let's rent a room.'"

"He never called me bitch," I amend with a smile.

She throws her arms up in irritation. "Whatever! He's a walking contradiction."

"Tell me about it." I sigh, perusing through the minimal information I can find on him.

Most of the information is the same—attended NYU, successful businessman by age twenty-five, parents both alive, has two siblings, comes from money, blah blah blah—but there's no dirt. No info on girlfriends—previous or current. No info on what made him the cold, heartless bastard that he is today.

I continue flicking through the pages while Hannah attempts to solve the riddle. "Maybe it's the classic case of a kindergarten crush."

"Huh?" I ask, looking up at her from my screen.

"You know, boys are mean to the girls they secretly like to hide their true feelings for," she explains.

"He has no feelings."

She shrugs. "Well, how about you test my theory out?"

My interest is piqued. "How?"

She taps her chin. "I've got an idea. If you can't beat 'em, join 'em."

"Care to be a little more specific?" Just as she attempts to clarify, I shoot up and exclaim, "Oh, oh!"

Hannah leans over, anxious to see what's got me so excited.

"There!" I jab at the screen. "This is the first picture I've seen of him with a woman."

Hannah turns her head to the side. "Or Cousin It. You can't see who she is. Is there a date on the photograph?"

Scrolling through, I see that there isn't. But that doesn't matter. "The clues are in the details, Han. Look at the way he's shielding her from the paparazzi. The way his hands are protectively wrapped around her. The anger on his face. He loves this woman." The revelation sinks low in my gut.

"You got all of that just by looking at this?" she asks, pulling a face at the screen.

"I need to find her. I need her to tell me what happened to make him such a monster."

"Have you thought that *she's* the reason why?"

"You're right. That bitch." I glare at the screen.

"Besides, the odds of you finding a slender, well-dressed brunette, without a name or face, are slim."

Transfixed on the photograph, I know that she's right. But at least I know he was human once because now, I'm just stuck with the monster.

Chapter Four

I can't believe I listened to Hannah, as her plan to trial if Mr. Fox likes me or not is ridiculous. But it's too late now.

After a weekend filled with copious amounts of ice cream and Bradley Cooper, I decided that this job is way too important for me to mess up. Apart from my boss, I actually love everything about it. I won't allow whatever is happening or not happening between Mr. Fox and me to affect my performance. I'm here to do a job, and that is all. I'm only participating in today's experiment to humor my best friend.

"You look hot," Hannah whispers from the side of her mouth.

"I look like a hooker," I amend, ignoring the looks of my male colleagues as we walk down the hallway.

"Hardly. You can barely see it."

The moment I make eye contact with Ken, I groan. I fiddle with the button on my blouse while Hannah smacks my hand away.

"Hi, girls," Ken says, jogging to catch up to us.

Mr. Fox's words from Friday night ring loudly, and I scowl. "Hi, Ken. Did you have a nice weekend?"

Hannah looks at me strangely while Ken smiles. "I did, except why did you bail Friday?"

I nearly fall over my feet. "I wasn't feeling too well. Sorry I left without saying goodbye."

"That's okay. As long as you're okay now. So, are you free for lunch?"

Internally flipping Tiger off, I nod. "I am."

"Great. Well, I usually go to this sushi bar down the road —" His eyes drop to my chest midsentence. It appears Hannah's plan has worked—but on the wrong person.

"Sounds great. I'll meet you at twelve thirty."

He looks surprised. As does Hannah. "Great, okay, see you then." Giving my chest one final glance, he turns around and walks back the way he came.

The daunting glass door haunts me, but I pull back my shoulders. "I'll talk later, Han." I lean forward, giving her a hug.

"Good to see your outfit works. Although, it's meant for Tiger, not your admirers. I want hourly updates."

Muting a laugh behind my hand, I push open the door, hating how loudly my heels click on the polished floor. Placing my bag on the desk, I see that I'm a couple minutes early. I use this time to gather my wits and feel comfortable with my wardrobe choice.

Hannah's genius idea involved a cream blouse and the blue bra Tiger gave me. If he remains unmoved, then I know he's a total heartless jerk, but if I get a rise out of him, then hooray for me. It's very childish and will probably backfire, but let the sinning begin.

When 8:02 a.m. ticks over, I take a deep breath and push open Mr. Fox's door with a staged confidence. He's sitting behind his desk, head buried in paperwork. As expected, he ignores me. At least the first part of the plan has gone how I expected.

Sauntering over to him, I place his coffee cup down on his desk without a word. I wait a second, but when he continues working, I take that as my cue to leave. Turning on my heel, I almost run to the door, but stop when Tiger decides to talk.

"Ms. Young."

I close my eyes, hating that I still respond to his voice this way.

"Yes," I reply, my back still turned.

"My two p.m. meeting. I would like you in attendance to take notes."

"Of course."

"And I'll be eating lunch in the office today. Could you please ensure I have turkey on rye at twelve forty-five p.m.?"

Great. There goes my lunch date with Ken.

"Not a problem." My back is still turned as the more, he speaks, the stupider I feel.

"Am I that repulsive you can't face me?" he asks a second later.

I refrain from saying yes, but instead turn slowly. The moment I do, his eyes drop to my chest, widening the moment he sees the color of my bra. It's subtle, but in the sunlight, the blue is highlighted underneath my sheer blouse. His pupils dilate, and my god, when he shuffles in his seat, I know that Hannah's plan has worked.

Mr. Unaffected appears totally affected and, for once, not guarding his emotions.

"Is there anything else I can help you with, sir?" I say, standing confidently as he checks me out.

When he lifts his eyes, his jaw firm, I melt. He swallows hard before replying. "T-that will be all."

I celebrate when I hear his stutter.

"Very well." I nod, unable to stop my smirk as I turn and walk to the door.

"Oh, Ms. Young?"

"Yes?" I reply midstep.

"Thank you for the coffee."

Now is not the time to gloat. When I do a little celebratory dance in the bathroom, then I can celebrate all I want. "You're welcome, sir."

The moment I close his office door behind me, I take a deep, victorious breath. Victory has never smelled this good.

Ken was disappointed I had to raincheck on lunch, but I promised it wouldn't happen again. I don't see anything happening with him, but I'm not turning down the offer to get to know him as a friend because this is what moving on entails.

But it's all business as usual as I'm sitting beside Mr. Fox, taking notes like he asked. I'm thankful I'm busy because the close proximity is killing me. But I focus on the task at hand because it distracts me from how good Mr. Fox smells.

The meeting is with an up-and-coming, kooky software developer who is trying to pitch his program which ingeniously detects and eradicates spyware before it has a chance to attack your computer. It's different to any that are out in the market at the moment, and I think his approach is quite clever. However, I don't think Mr. Fox agrees.

Fox Technologies is one of the biggest technology firms in the country. If there is a new craze in the latest apps, phones, operating systems, websites, software and hardware, you can bet someone from Fox Technologies designed it. Mr. Fox has truly seen it all, so as Marshall Powers is flipping through his eighth slide, I dare say Mr. Fox has seen enough.

As he glances down at his Rolex, he makes no secret that Mr. Powers is wasting his time. I can't help but feel for the guy.

"As you can see," Mr. Powers says, fumbling with the remote and skipping to the wrong slide. Mr. Fox sighs and leans back in his seat, twirling his gold pen between his fingers, unimpressed.

When he finds the correct slide, he continues. "As I was saying, this program is able to eradicate the spyware or adware ninety-eight point one percent faster than other security programs out there. Our impenetrable firewall and..."

But he's not permitted to finish. "Ninety-eighty point one percent?"

Mr. Powers pauses, looking over at me for guidance. I wish I could help, as I know what it feels like to be under Mr. Fox's microscope. "Y-yes," he stammers, pushing his thick-framed glasses up his nose.

Mr. Fox rocks back in his leather seat, tapping his pen on the table. I know what he's thinking even before he speaks. For someone who demands perfection one hundred percent of the time, ninety-eight point one percent isn't going to cut it.

"Thank you for sharing your vision, but I'm afraid I'm not interested. I simply cannot work with ninety-eighty point one percent. I demand excellence, Mr. Powers. If you can guarantee one hundred percent, then come see me, but now, you're simply wasting my time."

Ouch.

Mr. Powers doesn't hide his disappointment, but he smartly doesn't argue. "Thank you for your time, Mr. Fox." He acknowledges him with a brisk nod.

As I begin packing up, I feel his eagle eyes watching my every move. It appears Hannah's plan has worked, not that it makes a difference. I was stupid to think things could ever eventuate between us. It was a one-time deal. A one-night only fling. We are two very different people, and although our bodies think as one, our brains are certainly not on the same wavelength.

I think Mr. Powers's presentation was well presented and his ideas were ones Mr. Fox could work with. His figures were good, so was his outcome. He is someone Fox Technologies should be snapping up before someone else does. But that's not my call to make.

As I pack up my laptop, I sense Mr. Fox is still watching me closely. I've never had a good poker face, and now is no exception.

"Ms. Young." His curt voice is an indication that whatever he's about to say will probably piss me off. "Do you have something you'd like to add?"

Gathering my wits, I decide to express what I believe in as I feel Marshall Powers would be a very valuable addition to Fox Technologies.

"I don't mean to step out of line, Mr. Fox, but I think Mr. Powers's ideas are quite clever and advanced. The data which he presented is quite impressive and regardless of the percentage, I don't believe there ever will be a a hundred percent foolproof product, seeing as new hackers are arising every day, finding new ways to penetrate internet security."

When Mr. Fox shifts in his seat, I lower my eyes and bite my lip. I've overstepped a line. But the appreciation radiating from Mr. Powers makes it worthwhile.

"But that's just my opinion. The decision is ultimately yours," I conclude.

Mr. Fox silently mulls over what I've just said, steepling his long fingers underneath his chin. Mr. Powers looks over at me and gives me an indebted smile. The room is at Mr. Fox's mercy, waiting for him to speak. I sit calmly, but inside, my stomach is in knots.

Finally, he breaks the silence. "Mr. Powers, are you able to compile all the important parts of your presentation and email them to me?"

He almost falls over his feet. "Y-yes, of course."

"Good. I'll take another look over it, seeing as Ms. Young seems to believe in you."

My calm exterior almost slips, but I remain stone-faced, quietly packing up my notepad and supplies.

"Thank you so much, Mr. Fox. I really appreciate this opportunity. I will have the data in your inbox by tomorrow morning." Mr. Powers races over and shakes Mr. Fox's hand as he stands.

"You have Ms. Young to thank, Mr. Powers. She seems to see something in you that I cannot. Maybe she can see the perfection through the imperfection."

This time, I can't hold on to my composure and my pen skitters along the smooth, polished table. Mr. Powers saves it from tumbling to the floor, thankfully not paying too much attention to my clumsiness.

They bid each other farewell, while I try not to read too much into Mr. Fox's statement. As the boardroom door closes and Mr. Fox stands guard in front of it, I know I'm in trouble. My heart is still racing from his earlier comment, as I can't help but believe there is a double meaning behind it.

Hugging my laptop to my chest, I meet the eyes of my predator. He doesn't say a word, just continues dissecting me, tilting his head to the side. He looks remarkable in a light gray, three-piece suit. His whiskers are a little longer today, giving him a rougher-looking exterior—I like it.

"Is there anything further you require of me, sir?" I ask, unable to keep the tremble from my voice.

He leans against the wooden door, still silent, still watching me with an unreadable stare.

I can feel the static, the electrical current, the moment he folds his arms over his chest. We're high up, fifteen floors, and bounded by frosted glass. No one can help me up here. It's just my Tiger and me.

"Yes." The single word holds so much promise and chance. "Come here." Those two words however are spiked with nothing but danger.

My feet act before my brain can scream at me for going against better judgment, but the moment I'm enveloped in his signature fragrance, I tell my good sense to hit the road.

He makes no secret that he's looking at my breasts as his gaze drops to the front of my blouse. My chest begins rising and falling, my breathing choppy and winded. Pushing off the door, he strolls forward, stopping an inch away. His towering height dwarfs mine, but I won't allow that to deter me. I lift my eyes, a silent challenge.

"Does it please you to know that your antics have left my cock hard all day?"

"W-what?" I stammer, almost gagging on my tongue.

But he doesn't allow a moment to collect my thoughts. He latches on to my wrist and presses my hand against his semi-hard length. A stunned gasp catches in my throat—he's been hard all day? Because of me?

Answering my silent question, he guides my fingers to rub over the growing predicament in his pants. He feels incredible and memories of what he felt like inside of me, has me rubbing harder, not needing further encouragement.

"Congratulations, Bluebird, you've won this round." He gently removes his hand from mine, confident I will continue this show on my own, and I do.

Each movement has him growing harder and harder until

he's standing at full salute. Peering down timidly, my mouth waters and I'm mortified that I want a taste.

"You'll be the death of me," he hums, watching me as I envision dropping to my knees and blowing him in this fancy room.

I continue stroking him, quickening the pace, watching Tiger's mouth part, his eyes locked with mine. With steady fingers, he reaches forward and begins unsnapping the buttons on my blouse. When I'm halfway undressed, he parts the material with a finger, growling the moment he sees my blue bra.

"This looks even better than I imagined it would. And I can assure you, I've been imagining."

I try to stifle what his words are doing to me, but there's no point. Just like he said the moment we first touched, he knows what my body wants. And right now, it wants him. No matter how hard I try to hate him or stop myself from wanting him, I end up wanting him all the more. My traitorous body wins out yet again.

His finger slides along the silk of my bra cup, sashaying up and down at a deliriously slow speed. When he continues the movement, skating onto my bare skin, my flesh breaks out in an inferno of need, and I cup his erection firmly.

He grunts and arches into my hold. "You impressed me today, Bluebird. That smart mouth of yours always does."

"Thank you," I falter, sighing when he slips his warm hand into my bra.

His experienced finger traces around my areola, which has my nipples turning into rock-hard peaks. He rolls my left nipple, cupping my full breast and massaging me with a firm, desperate need. "I didn't appreciate these when I had the chance. Shame on me because they are fucking unbelievable. I better make up for lost time."

Before I have time to voice my approval, he yanks down my

bra cup, freeing my needy breast. Bending forward, he leisurely circles his wet tongue around my areola before drawing my nipple into his mouth. I cry out, my movement over his pants stilling, as all I can focus on is the way his mouth feels on me.

With one hand firmly affixed to my waist, he slithers the other down over my quivering stomach. He continues his journey until his hand ventures underneath my skirt, nestling between my legs. The dampness on the outside of my underwear highlights how ready I am. He doesn't speak, as our actions speak louder than words.

He continues sucking my breast, tonguing the underside and pulling my nipple until I am begging, pleading, needing more. My breast pops free as he drags his mouth away. "What do you want?"

How does he expect me to speak? He's everywhere, but it's not enough.

I groan impatiently, not wanting to talk.

"Tell me or so help me, God, I will leave you to take care of yourself," he warns, the threat sincere.

"I want to... come. Please." My voice is hoarse, sounding unlike me.

My answer pleases him. "Yes, you do."

He dives for my breast, flexing his fingertips around my waist and driving his finger up and down my entrance. The delicious contact is still over my underwear, but doing it this way feels wicked, almost like we're not breaking all the rules.

The more he sucks and strokes me, the wetter and needier I become; I couldn't mask my moans, even if I tried. When he begins circling two fingers over my clit and then dipping low, a tight knot begins to form in my belly. I recognize this feeling, and I want to embrace it with both hands. So I do.

Wedging my palm between us, I press my fingers over his, begging him to give me what I want. He groans around my breast, his warm breath triggering my knot to grow and grow. We begin an in sync rhythm, hurriedly rubbing over my quivering center, speeding up my impending orgasm only elicited by him.

When he bites my nipple and drums his finger over my clit, I can no longer hold on, and I cry out my release so loudly, I'm almost certain the entire floor can hear me coming. But regardless, I couldn't stop my explosion even if I tried.

It feels like minutes that tiny tremors rock my body, and I don't fail to notice the entire time, Tiger holds me close, offering my shaky legs the support I need. When I finally come down from my orgasmic bliss, my eyes pop open and I appreciate the sight of Tiger with his guard down.

"That was truly beautiful." He lifts the hand which was seconds ago between my legs and brushes a loose strand of hair off my brow. He smiles, a genuine smile, and the sight has me weak in the knees. "Are you okay?" he asks when I continue staring at him, speechless.

I nod, afraid of what my voice will sound like.

Giving my lips a brief kiss, he gently covers my exposed breast and draws my shirt closed. Is that it? We're not going to make use of that sturdy timber table?

"Don't look so disappointed. That was hot for me too."

But he's misread my regret. I'm grateful for the attention to detail, but right now, I just feel used.

I dress with uneven fingers, wondering what happens next.

Mr. Fox answers for me. "I won't be in for the rest of the afternoon. I have a few matters to attend to. I'll see you tomorrow."

Standing, speechless, I watch as he rearranges himself and straightens his tie. So that's it? He gives me a mind-blowing orgasm and expects me to return to work? Is he really going to disregard what happened between us yet again?

It appears so. "Good day, Ms. Young."

But I don't think so.

"Don't good day me," I spit, my anger shining. "You don't get to do that and then expect things to go back to normal, whatever the hell normal is with you!"

Mr. Fox smirks, which just infuriates me further.

I shove him in the chest and wave my invisible pom-poms when he bumps into the chair, taken off guard. "No, I am done being treated like this by men. My last boyfriend—"

However, I don't get to finish my sentence because Mr. Fox grips my throat and walks me toward the wall. He presses me against it, eyes on fire. "Don't ever mention him to me. *Ever*," he warns, his hot breath fanning my cheeks.

Is he... jealous?

"Understood?"

His hand is still around my throat, so I nod.

He opens his mouth as if wanting to say something but changes his mind at the last minute. He lets me go and storms out of the room, slamming the door behind him.

I don't know what just happened, but I intend to find out.

I'm feeling used, abused, and angry.

But this is no one's fault, not even Mr. Fox's fault. It's all mine. No one forced my hand; I voluntarily gave it up when I shoved it between my thighs.

What is the matter with me? I know Mr. Fox is trouble, but yet, I keep coming back for more. Well, no more. Today's indiscretion is the last of its kind, and this time, I mean it. No more falling victim to those eyes and our one-way attraction. I'm better than that.

I was hoping, by some miracle, Mr. Fox would come to me, professing his sincerest apologies for once again disregarding our actions, but he didn't. He instead pretended like nothing happened and treated me like a complete stranger.

I don't understand how he can switch his feeling on and off so quickly. But then I remember he doesn't have any.

He's left early—again, which has me wondering where he's going. It's just me and this empty office, which is why I'm ransacking Mr. Fox's desk, intent on finding... something. There has to be a reason why he is such an unfeeling asshole.

His office looks like a hurricane has torn through it and I suppose, in some ways, it has. I have searched through his filing cabinet and drawers, but have found nothing. But that doesn't deter me. I know he's hiding something.

When I find a folder of his previous PAs, I cringe because there is a name for every letter of the alphabet. The reason most were fired has me wondering why I haven't been added to this list. I've done far worse.

Suddenly, I get a sinking feeling in the pit of my stomach. Why am I different?

Hell-bent on finding out the reason, I toss file after file over my shoulder until I find mine. I examine over every inch of it, desperate to find a clue as to why I've not joined the laundry list of women who didn't make the cut.

I don't see anything of importance until I reach my work history and see a big red circle drawn around my ex-boss's name.

Why is she important to Mr. Fox? Does he know her?

Hannah's words play over in my mind. *"I do find it strange he hired you without even meeting you."*

I continue reading over my file, and when I see Mr. Fox took the liberty to do his own research, I know something is very wrong. It appears that he stalked my social media as there's a picture of Scott and me he printed out.

Why?

"Think," I mumble to myself, massaging my temples as I slump into Mr. Fox's chair.

The answer is staring me right in the face; I know it is. And when a beam of light catches something shiny on the filing cabinet, I realize it's staring me in the face—literally.

Jumping from the seat, I race over the glass duck which caught my eye days ago. I thought it looked out of place in here. Someone like Dylan Fox doesn't have these types of things in his office, which is why I pick it up and turn it from side to side, hoping it'll give me the answers I so desperately seek.

But I come up empty.

"Goddammit."

I go to place it back, but my thumb rubs over something raised at the bottom. Turning it over, I see it's a small gold plate which is engraved. The writing is small and in script, so I bring it over to the desk and place it underneath the lamp so I can see it clearer.

But I suddenly wish I didn't.

The duck falls from my hand, it shattering as it catches the corner of the desk. But I saw it, clear as day. The reason he hired me isn't because he was impressed with my resume. I doubt he even read it. He knew who I was the night we met, and he fucked me senseless.

He knew who I was all along when I had no idea who he was.

And who he is... is my ex-boss's husband.

To my darling husband, Dylan.
I'll love you for an eternity.
Your wife, Audrey.

Chapter Five

"I know you don't want to hear it, but this happened for a reason."

"And that reason would be?" I ask, needing her to fill in the blanks because I got nada.

Hannah sits up tall from the end of her bed. "It's to show you that some men are just plain bastards. You try and see the good in everyone, but any redeemable qualities Mr. Fox has, has been squashed under his huge ego and the need to treat people like shit. He's a bully. He's a narcissist jerk. The only things he loves are himself, his wallet, and his dick."

As she unsnaps the hair elastic from around her wrist and angrily pulls back her blonde hair into a high bun, I know this topic infuriates her as much as it does me.

I still can't believe Dylan is Audrey's husband. I mean, this isn't a coincidence. He hired me knowing who I was and what Scott did.

What I don't understand is why.

Is this his way to get one up on Audrey? To fuck me because she fucked Scott?

I feel sick.

"Here." Hannah passes me a bottle of water, but I wave it off because I'll just bring it back up.

"I don't get it. Why? Surely someone can't be this cruel?"

When Hannah doesn't reply, I know that someone can be.

"I feel so stupid," I sniff, refusing to cry. "He was doing this as some sort of revenge ploy? It was all fake."

"No, I've seen the way he looks at you. There is nothing fake about that."

But I don't believe it.

"That's it!" Hannah stands, tossing the bottle of water across the room. "We're going out."

"How about no," I grumble into the pillow as I bury my face into it.

However, when I hear coat hangers sliding across the railing, I know this isn't optional.

This is the worse idea—ever.

Being amongst loud music and even louder strangers is not the remedy to cure this ache in my chest.

There's only one explanation to why I feel like I want to carve out my heart—I've fallen for Dylan Fox. I knew he was trouble, but I willingly walked into the fire, prepared to be burned.

Hannah is dancing with some guy, but me, the only thing I'm dancing with is the devil as I throw back my seventh or maybe eighth shot of tequila. I can't believe I fell for his bullshit. I feel like such an idiot.

I slam the shot glass on the bar and twist my face as the tequila burns my throat.

"Another?"

Turning over my shoulder, I see a man with curly blond hair and piercing blue eyes smiling at me with a slanted grin. He is exactly the opposite of Dylan, which is why I nod.

"I would love one."

He flags down the bartender, ensuring our shoulders are touching. I like his confidence. "So what happened for you to want to drink the entire bar?"

I laugh, and it's a nice change from wanting to claw out my brain with an ice cream scoop. "How long you got?"

"For you? I got all the time in the world."

I smile because, damn, that's hot. A man who expresses how he feels instead of playing games because he's a narcissistic asshole.

The bartender places our drinks on the bar, and as I look at this handsome stranger, I throw caution to the wind and bend forward, licking the side of his neck. Before he can ask what I'm doing, I pepper his neck with salt, lick it deliberately slow before throwing back my shot.

His mouth is parted, which allows me to slip the sliver of lime between his lips and eat it from his mouth. I'm impressed as he deftly removes the lime rind in one smooth motion before kissing me deeply.

I don't know if it's the alcohol or the kiss, but everything spins quickly and I revel in the chaos, until I hear a voice which only heightens the madness.

"Good evening, Ms. Young."

The way his voice sends my senses into sensory overdrive and the way I'm left breathless, choking on my ragged breathing, all leads to one thing—Mr. Dylan Fox is here. Shitting on my already shitful day.

I make no attempt to stop kissing my surfer dude, however. And only deepen the kiss. And only when I'm content, do I pull away.

"Oh, I didn't see you there," I quip, relishing in a very pissed-off Mr. Fox.

"We're taking a walk." He grips my arm, but I yank it from his grasp.

"You can talk a walk," I rebuke, snuggling into my new beau's side. "I'm staying right here."

Dylan runs a hand through his hair which is snarled, unlike him. And when I take in his attire, I see his entire appearance is unkempt—unlike him.

"Baylee, I'm warning you..."

"Oh, fuck you," I snap, cutting him off. "You know what... I quit. You're nothing but a narcissistic, lying asshole who clearly needs a hug. I—"

I don't get to finish my rant because he picks me up and throws me over his shoulder, where he then storms his way through the sea of people who move out of the way quickly.

"Put me down!" I yell, kicking my legs, but to no avail.

The moment we're outside, he puts me down, only for me to slap his cheek.

"Don't you ever do that again! I am done with you, Dylan! I am done with your mixed signals! I am done with your games!"

He rubs his cheek and I see I've left a handprint behind.

"I'm sorry. You have every right to be angry."

"Don't you dare—" But stop dead in my tracks when I realize he just apologized and sounded genuine.

"I fucked up."

Again, I'm robbed of words because is he really admitting fault?

"I saw the duck. Well, I saw what's left of it. Can I please explain?"

I fold my arms across my chest, indicating I'm listening.

"Not here. My apartment is a few blocks away. Will you come with me?"

I should tell him no, but I know I'll forever regret it if I don't find out why. So I nod and follow as he leads the way. He doesn't make small talk, which I appreciate.

The moment we enter his building, I realize he just willingly invited me into his home. This means something because this is his personal sanctuary. But I don't get caught up in that and rather focus on the fact that this bastard used me for his own fucked up reasons.

It doesn't surprise me when we ride the elevator to the top floor and when the doors open, I see the entire level belongs to Dylan. Most would be impressed. I'm not.

He swipes a keycard over the panel, and when the doors open, I'm greeted with the most stunning view of the skyline. But this is all materialistic bullshit. What's the point of having riches if you can't enjoy it with the people you love?

I'm looking out the window when he appears with a bottle of water. "Take it," he gently orders when I eye it angrily.

Why is he being so nice?

I do, only because I want to wash down all the tequila I just drank. I wait for him to talk, but he seems nervous. So I decide to break the ice.

"What was I? Some game to you? A score to settle because your huge ego got bruised?"

He flinches, running a hand down his face. But I don't feel sorry for him. He didn't feel sorry for me when he treated me like dirt.

"At first, yes," he confesses, and I narrow my eyes, ready to break that expensive vase on the mantle over his head.

"So you knew who I was when you hired me?"

"Yes."

"And you hired me with the intent to fuck me to get back at your wife? She fucked my boyfriend, so you wanted to fuck his girlfriend?"

"Yes."

I respect he has been honest, but it still fucking stings. "How could you be so cruel?"

"I'm not proud of my actions, and if I could take it back, I would."

"Oh, that's nice to know."

"No, fuck, I didn't mean it that way."

But I've heard enough, and vomit rises—literal vomit.

With a hand over my mouth, I run down the hallway, thankful when I find the bathroom not too far away. I throw up into the toilet, wishing I could purge this sickness within.

"Baylee."

"Go away," I groan with my head buried in the toilet.

When I hear his footsteps along the floor, I know he's not going anywhere.

I feel a cool washcloth at the back of my neck, but as nice as it feels, I don't want his kindness. It's too late for that.

"I meant, if I could take back how we met, I would. But I don't regret that we did. Audrey filed for divorce months ago, but I never signed the papers. I wanted to punish her and not give in. And when I found out what she did with your ex-boyfriend, I—"

He sighs, appearing to find the right words.

"I needed to hurt her how she hurt me. But I never told her about us because the moment I met you, I knew it was... more. You're the only woman to challenge me in every possible way. And although it drove me crazy, I liked it."

I feel my cheeks heat, and that unwanted, familiar fire

begins to smolder in my stomach. But no, he doesn't get to do that.

Pushing him off me, I lift my head from the toilet, and when I see nothing but honesty reflected in his eyes, I realize he's telling me the truth.

"How can I trust you?" I ask. "What you did, it's unforgivable. You used me. Go back to your *wife*, Mr. Fox. You deserve one another."

"I'm not interested in her, and anyone else—"

I don't allow him to finish, as his statement cements what a huge asshole Mr. Fox really is. "Oh, you son of a bitch! I get it. No need to spell it out for me. I am just one of the many women you've probably fucked and forgotten all about. It's my fault I actually thought you liked me."

And then, there was silence, and I instantly regret my overshare. I need to leave.

Standing up, I ignore how the room spins and make my way toward the door.

"Baylee, please wait. Don't go."

But I am done with this man. With his games. With him screwing with my mind.

Just as I'm about to open the door, he says something which ends my resolve because they're the words I've wanted to hear since the moment we met.

"I'm not interested in anyone, but *you*. And if you'll let me, I'd like to start again. I'd like you to see the real me."

I can feel him at my back. My body responds to him in ways I don't understand. I should hate him, but I don't.

"I'm fucked up. I know that. But when I'm with you, I feel... like someone I want to be."

My heart clenches at his words, but my brain is reminding me what he did.

"I can't, Dylan. What you did—"

"I know," he replies, gently wrapping an arm around my waist. "I'll spend however long it takes begging for forgiveness. Give me a chance. Please."

I want to. I really do. But how can I trust him?

"I'll see you at the office."

"I quit," I remind him, basking in his warmth.

"I don't accept your resignation. I'll see you bright and early, Ms. Young. And that's an order."

And only then does he let me go.

Chapter Six

I 'm clearly crazy.

There's no other explanation as to why I'm here, about to exit the elevator and stroll into work like nothing happened.

The weekend didn't provide any clarity. I'm still just as confused. But what I do know is that saying goodbye to Dylan is something I don't want. I can't walk away from this.

Hence, why I'm clearly crazy.

This is a dumpster fire waiting to happen, but it's too late now.

I exit the elevator, and the office is in full swing as I've purposely arrived late. I walk through the office, greeting my colleagues as I normally would. The moment I'm about to take a seat behind my desk, the phone rings and I see Mr. Fox is paging me.

This was a bad, very bad idea.

Taking a calming breath, I enter his office, preparing myself for everything, but when all I see are red roses, I realize I haven't prepared for anything. I close the door, unsure if I'm hallucinating or not. But when Dylan appears from behind the endless bunches of roses, I know that this is really happening.

"What?" It's all I can articulate.

Dylan offers me the bunch of roses he holds. "You're late."

A laugh escapes me. "So you decided to buy out every florist in the city as punishment?"

The roses smell lovely, but I don't get it. "What's going on?"

"I wanted to express my sincerest apologies for being a dick, hence the—" And he extends out his hand to the roses.

"A dozen would have sufficed."

"Nonsense." And there he is, the arrogant jerk I've grown to—love?

No, not love, but at least like. And for that to happen, we have to start again.

"Thank you for the roses, but it's going to take more than that."

His handsome face drops. "Name it, and it's yours."

Placing the roses on his desk, I open my bag and produce something I've been working on all weekend. I offer it to him.

He accepts, reading it over and I see it—he knows what I want.

"Very well, Ms. Young. Take a seat."

The way he says my name heats me from head to toe, but I remain unaffected as I sit.

He, too, takes a seat, reading over my resume.

This is the only way we can start again. For us to start over.

"I see you worked for Audrey Denis."

I nod, sitting up tall.

He watches me closely. "I heard she's a real bitch."

I stifle a chuckle. "I heard her husband is even worse."

Dylan's mouth twitches. "Ex-husband."

I can't hide my surprise because he did it. He signed the

divorce papers. I don't want to get my hopes up that he did so because of me.

"Your resume is very impressive. How are you at taking orders?"

The walls suddenly close in on me.

"Because I demand perfection and exercise control in everything I do."

He stands, removing his jacket, while I swallow past the lump in my throat.

"Do you think you can handle that?"

I remain posed and nod coolly. "Yes. But as for taking orders, it all depends on what you demand."

"Oh, I am very demanding, Ms. Young."

"So am I."

He saunters toward me while I cross my legs. His eyes instantly focus on the heels I'm wearing—the same ones I wore when he fucked me senseless.

"I don't like to lose."

"Well, I like a challenge."

His lips twitch. "Seems like a disaster waiting to happen."

Before I can reply, he drops to his knees before me, and the gesture touches me—he surrenders to me.

"But I'm game if you are. The job is yours if you want it."

"Oh, I want." I'm suddenly not talking about the job.

Dylan kisses up my leg slowly, his devilish mouth sending goose bumps all over me. He takes his time, and I watch because the sight is simply hot. He carefully shifts the hem of my dress, but I grip his wrist, shaking my head.

"But I don't sleep with the boss."

"Then you're fired," he says, lips pressed against my inner thigh.

"But that would be an unfair dismissal? Whatever would HR say?"

"Fuck HR."

He works his way up my body and slams his mouth to mine. Our kisses are laced with nothing but desire, but the undertone is now different—it's paved with a possibility of new beginnings.

I yank at his hair as I circle his tongue with mine and just as he walks his hand up my thigh, I pull away.

"I accept your terms, Mr. Fox."

I push him back, relishing in the way he falls onto the carpet, surprised I said no. But it's going to take a lot more than some roses and kind words to forget what he did.

"Can I get you a coffee?"

He doesn't bother rising from the floor. Nor does he hide his erection. For once in this relationship, I'm the one in control. How the tables have turned.

"Yes, black."

"Anything else?" I ask sweetly while he clenches his jaw.

"No, Ms. Young. That'll do. For now."

I smile and go to turn but am stopped when he adds, "You've won this round... Bluebird."

And I finally ask the question which has lingered on my tongue since we met. "Why Bluebird?"

His reply was not what I was expecting. "Bluebirds are a symbol of hope, renewal and... love."

My heart swells because this proves that Dylan is telling me the truth about feeling an instant connection.

"I've won the entire game... Tiger. Try and keep up." Turning over my shoulder, I blow him a kiss and watch as his desire for me grows tenfold.

I leave his office, the victor, something I didn't think I'd ever be when Mr. Fox was involved. But victory has never tasted this good because, like a boss, I just won this game.

I look forward to the rematch, however, because I know there's more to come...

Subscribe to my Newsletter: https://tinyurl.com/mvjjk6k2

About the Author

Monica James spent her youth devouring the works of Anne Rice, William Shakespeare, and Emily Dickinson.

When she is not writing, Monica runs her own business, but she always finds a balance between the two. She enjoys writing twisted AF stories, hoping to terrify her readers...just a little.

She is a bestselling author in the U.S.A., Australia, Canada, France, Germany, Israel, and the U.K.

Monica James resides in Melbourne, Australia, with her Unicorn, and her three crazy cats. She is slightly obsessed with red lipstick, heels, and crime documentaries, and is *that* person who always runs late.

Connect with

MONICA JAMES

Website: authormonicajames.com
Facebook: facebook.com/authormonicajames
Twitter: twitter.com/monicajames81
Goodreads: goodreads.com/MonicaJames
Instagram: @authormonicajames
TikTok: @authormonicajames
BookBub: http://bit.ly/2E3eCIw
Amazon: https://amzn.to/2EWZSyS
Reader Group: http://bit.ly/2nUaRyi
Newsletter: https://tinyurl.com/mvjjk6k2

www.ingramcontent.com/pod-product-compliance
Lightning Source LLC
Chambersburg PA
CBHW072149130726
47909CB00004BB/1396